# THE GOOD DETECTIVE

*A Mystery*

# H.R.F. Keating

SCRIBNER

New York   London   Toronto   Sydney   Tokyo   Singapore

SCRIBNER
1230 Avenue of the Americas
New York, NY 10020

First Scribner edition 1995
First published in Great Britain by Macmillan London Limited

SCRIBNER and design are trademarks of Simon & Schuster Inc.

Manufactured in the United States of America

1   3   5   7   9   10   8   6   4   2

Library of Congress Cataloging-in-Publication Data
Keating, H. R. F. (Henry Reymond Fitzwalter), 1926–
The good detective: a mystery/H. R. F. Keating.—1st Scribner ed.
      p.   cm.
Originally published: Great Britain: Macmillan London.
                I.   Title.
        PR6061.E26G63   1995
   823'.914—dc20                    95-9078            CIP

ISBN 0-684-81522-2

# THE GOOD DETECTIVE

# 1

Ned French, Assistant Chief Constable (Operations)
Edward French, City of Norchester Police, never let himself be late. Nor anyone else. But he had woken so long
past his usual hour – no one had shared his bed – that,
just snatching a quick shave, he had had to abandon
breakfast, the paper, even the radio.

'At last,' his secretary said as he came striding in.

'What do you mean *at last*? One minute to nine. I'm
not late.'

'No. But you're always here fifteen minutes early,
twenty.'

'What if I am? The time I choose to arrive's my own
business. And I'll thank you not to take advantage.'

'Sorry, I'm sure. But the Chief wants to see you. Conference with Detective Chief Superintendent Grundy.'

'What? Now? Straight away?'

'That's what his secretary said. *As soon as he comes in.*'

'Better see what it's about then.'

Going out, he turned.

'Sorry if I snapped. Truth is I overslept. Been in a hell
of a rush ever since.'

'That's all right.'

Scarcely audible mutter.

'So who's a sulky, unforgiving little bitch? Do I take
it, then, you won't want dinner this evening?'

A moment's pause. A spreading perkiness.

'Well, okay, yes. If you do.'

1

'Right. Same place as before, Golden Goose at Markham. Same time. And, I trust, same afterwards. Unless something comes up.'

'I was at the Chamber of Commerce dinner last night,' the Chief Constable said, contriving to get his almost white eyebrows to bristle, 'and a prominent businessman in the city – I shan't name him – told me he had actually met face to face at a party, at a drinks party in a friend's house, a pair of brothers he understood to be London criminals. Criminals of the first water. Established here in Norchester. In one of those big houses in the South End. Corrigan, that was the name. Do either of you know anything about these men? Do you even know they're here? Why haven't I been kept informed?'

'Nothing to inform you of, sir,' Ned answered. 'Not as yet. We can hardly prevent people coming here to live, if they so choose.'

'So you do know about them. Well, who exactly are they? What sort of records have they got, these Corrigan brothers?'

'Cousins, as a matter of fact, sir. And not quite of – what was it you said? – of the first water. But nasty enough. They might rank third or fourth in London now. Protection rackets mostly. Not afraid to have plenty of grievous bodily harm inflicted. I had some dealings with them when I was in the Met. There are three Corrigans actually, not two. Martin, known as Marty, Bartholomew or Barty, and Francis.'

'Farty.'

Big George Grundy, beard shadow already darkening ruddy-flushed cheeks, leant sharply forward. Delight all too apparent. Opportunity to make the incomer from the South look some sort of a sissy.

'Yes, he's called that,' Ned said. 'An unpleasant habit he has. Which he takes no pains to control, in any circumstances. I very much doubt if he was at the drinks

2

party, sir, where your Chamber of Commerce friend was so shocked. The other two are a good deal more presentable. Martin is the brains and Bartholomew' – he took some pleasure in drawing out the syllables for Grundy's benefit – 'is what you might call the will. The will to make their particular shit-heap higher than any other.'

'And you're telling me these people are building such a – such a shit-heap here? Here in Norchester?'

'Not a great deal of evidence as yet, sir. They've acquired a club and a couple of restaurants. Legit places, but nothing else so far. It's too early to know whether they've just come here to lie low or whether they mean to get up to their old tricks.'

'I'd like to see them try, that's all,' Grundy exploded. 'We know how to deal with flash Londoners here.'

'Not a great deal of evidence, Mr French? But just exactly how much? What haven't I been made privy to?'

'Very little, sir, as I said. And perhaps nothing more to come that you should be – what was it? – made privy to.'

'Mr Grundy, you agree with that assessment?'

Grundy pressed his heavy lips into a pout. A long moment to work out the best answer.

'Suppose I do, sir. If Mr French has fully put me in the picture.'

'Oh, and why is it him who is putting you in the picture, and not the other way about? And why should there be any doubt that he has? I won't have any lack of co-operation between any of my officers, be they newcomers or old Norchester hands.'

'I've been careful to tell Mr Grundy everything I've come to know, sir. I'd consider it less than my duty if I failed to. But the fact is that our knowledge of the Corrigans' activities happens to come from a man who was one of my informants back in London.'

'A nasty little snout,' Grundy put in.

3

'Well, a snout certainly. But not altogether nasty. And not so little. The Corrigans ran, perhaps still run, a number of clubs and restaurants in London, apart from their protection rackets. And my informant, no more than a general hanger-on when I first got hold of him, rose up in their organization. He used mostly to look after the legit side. Well placed to know what was going on, though. So I'm happy to have him to tap up here. Learn just what, if anything, our friends have in mind.'

'Well, I don't like it, Mr French. I'll be plain with you. I don't like the idea of London criminals coming here and thinking they can play havoc with us simple provincials. We've still some notion of the Queen's peace in Norchester.'

'Quite right, sir,' Grundy chimed in.

'I don't like having the Corrigans here, sir, any more than you do,' Ned said. 'But it's always possible they've simply made things too hot for themselves in London, either with the Met or with some other firm with more muscle, and have come here to live the quiet life.'

'But they've acquired that club, yes? No doubt a disreputable establishment? What's it called? Do I know it?'

'It is disreputable, yes, sir. Classy in a way, but, yes, disreputable. Dope peddlers use it, that sort of thing. It's called Psmith's.'

George Grundy tugged an old envelope from his pocket, scribbled.

'That's Smith with a silent P at the start, George,' Ned said.

He received the glare he expected.

'And you've heard nothing, nothing at all, Mr French, about these people going in for protection here? Or anything else we wouldn't want? Running girls?'

'Too much of that going on already, if you ask me,' Grundy put in. 'I've said before. We should come down a sight harder on every whore in the city.'

4

'I thought it'd been agreed what we do about that,' Ned countered sharply. 'I don't want detectives spending half their time in court on tuppenny-ha'penny cases.'

'Tuppenny-ha—'

'That's enough, Mr Grundy. There's no point in arguing it all out again. As you said, Mr French, we have arrived at our policy on that somewhat contentious matter, and so long as the Police Committee are happy I see no reason to make a change.'

'Lot of lily-livered liberals.'

'That's as may be, Mr Grundy. But they're the people I have to report to, and the ones I depend upon for my finances. And, speaking of finance ... Mr French, are you making heavy payments to this source of yours?'

'No, sir. This is a fellow I've known for years. It was quite a surprise bumping into him in Norchester in fact. So our relations are strictly on an old acquaintance basis, with an occasional reference to a certain weakness of his. Touch of public toilets grottiness. How I got hold of him in the first place.'

'Bloody poofter. Doesn't surprise me.'

'Well, Mr Grundy, we've all dirtied our hands from time to time to find out what was going on among the criminal fraternity, and at least we're not spending taxpayers' money here. I tell you I don't at all like the current fashion for these substantial payments to informants. In my day they were lucky to get a pound note and a drink.'

'More than they deserve.'

'I'm inclined to agree with you there, Mr Grundy. But is this source of yours, Mr French – I take it you're not anxious to tell us any more about him than you have – is he entered on the Register?'

'No, sir, he's not. I didn't think it necessary. As I say, all I've learnt from him since we happened to meet has been, as it were, friend to friend.'

'Some of us obey the rules,' Grundy muttered.

5

'Mr Grundy, if anyone is to point that out it will be myself.'

'Yes, sir. But when such a lot's made of going by the book nowadays . . .'

'I'm very glad to hear a lot is being made of going by the book, as you put it. I don't want to find any officer in my force has stepped out of line. I don't want to hear that telephone there ring and have to explain to someone in the Home Office something that— That cannot be explained.'

'I think you can rest assured,' Ned put in, 'there's nothing going on in CID to upset the Homebodies.'

'Well, I should hope not, Mr French. And furthermore I don't want to wake up one morning and find the City of Norchester Police headlined in the press. Did you see the reference in *The Times* this morning to possible police mishandling of that ecology bombing case years ago?'

'What I saw in my *Northern Journal*, sir?' Grundy offered. 'The Wildfire for Wildlife case? They had a long story about it. Saying the woman who planted the bomb that killed all those children never did it. Typical piece of press sniping.'

Wildfire for Wildlife.

The past knocking suddenly at the door.

Why the hell had he slept so late? Not seen the paper, heard the radio?

'Shirley, you have the *Northern Journal*, don't you? You got it there?'

'I've lent it to Cindy, old Grunty-grunty's daughter-in-law. Met her in the canteen.'

'She the PC I sometimes see in his office? Tall girl, plenty of tits and bum?'

'If you like to put it like that, yes. She works in Fingerprints. But if you want the paper specially, I can go and ask for it back. I wasn't all that keen to lend it.'

6

'No. No, don't do that. I don't want everybody to . . . Listen, did you read a piece they had about Heather— About that woman who was convicted years ago in the Nottingham bombing case?'

'No. Oh, wait. There was something. Them saying she didn't do it after all? Something about wildlife rights? I didn't read it all.'

'But enough to know the strength of it? Or did you just skim the first paragraph?'

'No, I read more than that. They were saying the real person who planted that bomb – it killed some children too – they said this man had committed suicide not long ago, and some friends of his say he told them that he was the one who did it and not the woman. Terrible, really, to have let her – did you say her name was Heather something? – to have left her to rot in prison all those years. But you sure you don't want to see it for yourself? It'd be no trouble to get it from Cindy.'

'No. No, I just wanted to know if there was any real substance in the story.'

'Hey, but didn't you say once you began in the police in Nottingham? You have something to do with the case back then?'

'I was in Nottingham then, yes.'

# 2

Pure chance that Heather Jonas had been left to Palmy Palmer and himself that night. After the preliminary sort-out she had hardly rated among the thirty-odd suspects. She had been thought of as the merest hanger-on among the Wildfire for Wildlife lot camped beside that stretch of the Tottle Brook. The only place in England, or in all Britain, or, was it, in all Europe where the Ison's Kingfisher nested.

Ison's Kingfisher.

Extraordinary how after all those years the name came back. When nowadays he scarcely ever gave the business so much as a passing thought.

At dawn that day bulldozers in the howling orange livery of – another name coming back – Smart Construction had gone in and torn up that whole stretch of land on the edge of the city. Bushes and trees ruthlessly dumped into the little struggling stream. Then, some time in the afternoon, there had been the bomb. The one that had killed Reardon Smart, pushful chairman of Smart Construction, as he got into his car at his luxury home in The Park. Killed not just Reardon Smart. But three five-year-olds too, arriving at that moment for the Smart kid's birthday party. Three killed, and how many others injured? Twelve? Thirteen? Something like that.

So the outrage had come in a sudden, mounting, unstoppable tidal wave. Not of green, cold sea-water but of red-hot, immediate, unthinking, widespread anger.

8

The protesters out at that ramshackle camp had been arrested within the hour, as much for their own safety as for questioning. But each of them had been questioned. Someone had to be charged. That had been imperative. Whichever one of them had actually planted that bomb under Reardon Smart's car. And, if at all possible, charges had to be brought as well against the bomb maker or makers and anybody who had in any way actively assisted. An announcement that someone, or more people than one, was to be brought to court needed to be made. Fast. To contain the public anger. And – little though this was said aloud – to make bright the image of the force.

They had started on Heather Jonas, the two of them, some time after 3 a.m. when they had finished with another of the less likely protesters. No careful noting of the exact time, though. This was long before the days of the Police and Criminal Evidence Act, and the scrupulous tape-recording of every interview. No business of date and time and *Present, Heather Margaret Jonas and arresting officers, Detective Sergeant Palmer and Detective Constable 375 French*. Long before the days, too, when confessions began to be automatically looked on as doubtful until supported by hard evidence. No, back then, unless a suspect was an obvious nutter, some sort of pathological attention seeker, a confession was seen as just that. The admitting of guilt.

Not that they had expected anything of the sort from Heather Jonas. There on the other side of the table in that interviewing room out at—

Jesus, he could not remember now which police station it had been, certainly it wasn't at Force HQ at Burnstump Park. Only the really likely suspects were under interrogation there. By detective chief superintendents, detective superintendents, detective chief inspectors. No, Heather Jonas and other peripherals had been whisked away to wherever there happened to be spare cells, and she had eventually been led into the Interview Room there, wherever it was. To face Palmy Palmer and himself. Palmy, old-style detective sergeant, only just risen then as high as he would ever get, mucking along, just about making sure his arrests record was acceptable, pulling in the easy ones, letting the tough ones go if he was safe from interference from above. But with his sudden areas of prejudice, illogical, fixed, vituperative.

Among them feminists and environment fanatics.

Like Heather Jonas. Somewhere in her thirties, though looking more from the sleepless hours ever since she had been pulled in. White-faced. No, grey-faced. And, of course, no cosmetics. Hair in a total mess. A slash of a mouth, bloodshot eyes wide with fear or strain. And her clothes not helping. Mud-stained jeans buried in aged mud-covered rubber boots, a roll-neck pullover in some indeterminate shade between green and brown, with a pulled thread making a dangling loop just below her left breast. He could see that still now, as it all began coming back to him.

Palmy, of course, had begun with a couple of old tricks. The long, silent look of contempt, meant by its very length to start the worm of unease wriggling. And then the cigarette casually lit, luxuriously drawn on, and the puff of grey smoke from the depths of the lungs rolling out towards the victim. And, yes, it had been plain that this particular victim was a smoker. That she longed for that simple comfort.

Not that he had felt the least twinge of sympathy for her. His first couple of years in the force had cured him of sympathy. He had been conned too often by a cheerful grin, or a look of dull hopelessness. Only to find the indulgence either one had brought repaid by the same criminal behaviour repeated in the same fashion. Times without number. So well before he had got into the CID he had seen his path as being to do what he was paid to do. To clobber the law-breakers. And not to listen to the wiles, the sob stories. A lesson he kept to heart even today. *Don't give the buggers one inch.* His motto.

At last Palmy had begun.

'Right, who was it then?'

'Who...? I don't understand.'

'Oh, yes, you do. And you know who it was, too. Now, make it easy for yourself. Just tell us who put it there, and you can go back to your cell and I'll tell them to let you sleep. Bring you a nice cup of tea. Bit salty, the one they brought you before, was it? Funny how that happens.'

'But I—I don't know what you're talking about. Who put what where? I don't understand. I don't—Oh, God, I'm so tired.'

'You'll be a hell of a sight tireder before I've done, if you go on that way. I've got all night, and all day too if I want. And when I get to feel tired I can go for a nice little kip. But don't think you can, my girl. You're here until you tell us what you know.'

'Know? I don't know anything. I don't understand. I don't understand anything.'

'Oh, yes. Very clever. Don't know nothing. Didn't see anything. Didn't hear anything. Well, it won't wash with me, lady. You saw. You heard. You damn well know who did it, and the sooner you bloody well tell me, the better it'll be for you.'

A blank face opposite them then. The blankness of the exhaustion she had pleaded? Or the blankness of obstinacy?

He remembered that face. Saw it now. And remembered how seeing it he had repeated to himself his hard-won creed. *Don't give the buggers one inch.*

So eventually Palmy had started in with the rat-a-tat-tat questions, another old technique. Hammer, hammer, hammer. Hammer enough at just one spot and something gives.

11

'Who put it there?'

'Who had it?'

'Who was it?'

'Come on, come on, who was it?'

'Who was it?'

'Who put it there?'

'Who?'

'Who?'

'Who?'

'Who?'

On and on. But no result. What worked well enough with the minor criminals Palmy was used to had done nothing here. The dull, blank face had swung from side to side, as if each question had been a slap to one cheek or the other.

As they well might have been.

All Palmy could think of then was to move on to another of his tricks. A dirtier one.

'Hands on the table!'

'What? What hands?'

'Your hands, you stupid bitch. On the table. In front of you. And quick about it, or . . .'

The shouted threat was enough.

Bemusedly she had brought her hands up from her lap and rested them in front of her.

'Flat. Flat. Flat down. You bitch.'

This time she understood. At least what she was being told to do. However little she must have known why.

Her two hands spread palms down on the pale cigarettes-burnt surface of the bolted-to-the-floor table. Palmy standing up and taking from his pocket – Jesus, in those days he had worn a tweed jacket – his pair of handcuffs.

'Now, we'll have a bit of co-operation. Who put that bomb there?'

'Bomb? I don't—'

The handcuffs, held at one end in Palmy's fist, whistling down. Hardly any noise as they struck the nearer of the two hands planked there on the table. But Heather Jonas had screamed. A short, sharp jab of a scream. A moment later a dull red line of bruising showed itself across the outstretched fingers on the table.

'I asked you: who put that bomb under the car?'

'But I—'

The whistle of the descending metal rings. The dull sound as they landed.

This time, knowing what was coming, Heather did not scream. But a hiss of pain told how effective the treatment was.

'Please. Please, stop. Stop. I—What do you want to know? What? What? Please.'

'What do I want to know, you conniving shit? I want an answer to what I've been asking you for God knows how long. Who put that bomb under the car?'

'But— But— What bomb? What bomb, please? I don't—'

Palmy had raised the handcuffs again, well above his shoulder.

But that was the moment he himself had intervened. Not out of pity. God forbid. But because he thought he had suddenly grasped what the situation was. Heather Jonas, it had abruptly struck him, simply did not know about the bomb. She wasn't acting dumb, he had thought. Snatched by the mob-handed squad that had driven, brakes screeching, tyres yowling, out to the makeshift camp beside Tottle Brook, bundled into one of the vans, she might not actually have heard about the bomb. Palmy, in his slapdash, unthinking way, had, until a moment before, never once said precisely that a bomb had been used.

So then he had pushed forward across the table himself.

'This afternoon – yesterday afternoon, God damn it – someone put a bomb under Reardon Smart's Rover

13

down at his house and killed him. Now, are you going to talk?'

But she had not talked. She had sat there, her hands still flat on the table in front of her, a few slow beads of blood oozing up where Palmy's second blow had crossed the first. Plainly turning over in her sleep-deprived mind what she had just learnt.

Even Palmy had realized she was thinking. Even he must have worked out that since she – as we both thought at that point – had only just heard about the bomb and what it had done it might pay simply to leave her to think.

He himself had sat there, looking at her, supposing she would be going over in her head who among the Wildfire for Wildlife lot might have possessed a bomb, could have taken it to Reardon Smart's house in The Park and slid it beneath his gleamingly polished car. Perhaps she would be asking herself – he had thought – whether, for all the Wildfire for Wildlife bluster she presumably believed in, it was after all right to kill for the cause. Perhaps she was in the grip of a dilemma. Tell what she knew of her comrades, or protect them?

At last she had spoken.

'That bastard Reardon Smart, he deserved to die. He bloody well deserved to die.'

Palmy gave a sudden loud gasp. Ridiculously, absurdly loud. Then, taking one swift step behind her, he grabbed her hair and jerked it savagely back.

'You fucking bitch. It was you, wasn't it? You, all along. You put that bomb there. Christ.'

And, even as she shrieked in pain, he had thought – the moment had lain like a buried casket in his mind ever since – that Palmy had jumped to the wrong conclusion. Heather had not, at that instant, actually confessed. Palmy had simply leapt on the words she had said as meaning more than they actually did.

Then, with her hair still tugged fiercely back, Palmy had pulled her to her feet and hit her.

It had been cunningly and cruelly done.

Handling the clever-dick petty criminals he customarily dealt with, Palmy had learnt how to soften them up with something more than threats. He knew just how to plant a savagely painful blow where it left no lingering mark.

One blow. Two. Three.

Then Heather's face – it had seemed to him – had taken on a look of blanked-out nothingness. The same sort of all-pervading brute obstinacy it had worn at the start.

It was at that point he had become convinced – or almost convinced, had it been? – that everything that had gone before had been total play-acting. Palmy was right. Heather Jonas had known about the bomb. Known all about it. For the one and simple reason that it had been she herself who had pushed it under that gleaming rich man's Rover.

From that point on the interrogation had become altogether different. No longer had he been content to let Palmy get on with the process of battering the truth out of someone who till then had seemed a minor suspect. He had taken his full share of the questioning, never hesitating to add an extra one to Palmy's. To try a new twist. And the questioning had been relentless. Unsparing. With the two of them glowingly aware that there in front of them was the woman who had planted the bomb. The woman who had not cared – such single-minded perversity was almost unbelievable – who else it might kill besides the man who had ordered the destruction of some piffling wild bird's habitat.

Looking back now, he could see they should have put Heather straight into the hands of the top brass. But he had been young, and the thought had sprung up that here was his big chance. He was going to be the man – well, Palmy would want his share – who had triumphed in the Wildfire for Wildlife bombing case.

Of course, in the end the top brass had secured almost

all the credit. He had been junior enough and innocent enough then not to see how that was inevitable. Yet, as time had gone by, being one of the two who had actually broken the Wildfire for Wildlife bomber had done him a lot of good.

It could have done Palmy as much good, too, if he had been up to building on it. But Palmy had stayed locked in his old methods, his old dodging of responsibilities, his old trick of always taking the easiest way out. So Palmy – what had happened to him in these past few years? – had remained a detective sergeant. Lucky most probably to keep that place in CID. Some sparks of the glory that had briefly come to them that night must have helped. While he himself . . . Well, he'd had a bloody good career. No need to be modest about facts.

Of course, Heather Jonas had not cracked at once. All she would do at first was to repeat that Reardon Smart deserved to die. At first, and for a weary hour and more afterwards. But they had had the scent of her guilt flaring their nostrils. It would have taken a tougher suspect by far than that mixed-up creature to resist.

*Don't give the buggers one inch.* His creed had stood him in good stead while Heather Jonas had endlessly repeated that one cry of defiance. Even when Palmy resorted once more to his cunningly applied violence she had wriggled and contradicted herself. She had lapsed again into long dully obstinate silences. She had shouted and wept and pleaded to be left in peace. At last watching Palmy, still shouting and storming, bring his heavy shoe stamping down on Heather's thin old rubber boot, he had seen what might unlock her.

The kindness card. Play it ruthlessly, if there's any chance it will work. Play it for all it's worth. In an instant switch from the tough to the ultra-sympathetic. Go the whole hog. *Don't give the buggers one inch.*

'Heather, listen now. Nobody's saying you meant to kill those kids. I'm sure myself you'd no idea they'd be

16

there. But we can't know that was all a mistake till you tell us just exactly what you did do down there, can we? So, come on, love. Let's just have the simple truth, eh? Just simply tell me all about it.'

'The children. No, that shouldn't have happened.'

And then, then, she had lifted her head proudly – yes, that very word had come into his mind as he watched her – had lifted her head proudly and said, 'But Reardon Smart deserved to die. And I killed him. Yes, me. It was me.'

# 3

'You're miles away.'

'What— Yes. Yes, I was thinking.'

'About the – what was it? – Wild-something for Wild-life case?'

'Yes, that.'

'Well, do you think she's actually been not guilty all along, Whatever-her-name-was?'

'Heather Jonas. No, she was guilty all right. I was the one who originally interrogated her, as a matter of fact. Me and a DS Palmer. And— Well, methods were a bit different in those days. But she confessed all right. Told us straight out she planted that bomb. Pleaded Guilty at her trial.'

'But then . . . This man, the one who committed suicide and told his friends that he was the one who did it?'

'Not there to be talked to now, is he? And someone who'd give up the game like that, I wouldn't call his evidence exactly reliable.'

'So you think this is being all cooked up by the papers? Or the telly? That story mentioned there was going to be a programme next month in the *Justice Watch* series.'

'That says it all, sweetheart. Professional cop baiters.'

'Yes . . . Well, that's what they say here at HQ. But then they're bound to, aren't they?'

'*Justice Watch* hasn't been right every time, my girl. The great British public forgets that. Nobody wants to

18

hear the police sometimes get murderers bang to rights. Doesn't make a juicy enough story.'

'Yeah, I suppose so. But . . .'

'Well? But what?'

'Well, *Justice Watch* has shown up miscarriages before, hasn't it?'

'Okay. It has. But not as often as they've got it wrong. Or three-parts wrong. And are we going to get any work done today, or not? Tell me that.'

'Mr French. Well, this is a surprise. I trust you enjoyed your meal. And the young lady? May I have the honour . . .?'

He looked up at the man hovering solicitously over them. The unhealthily pale face with the ever-flickering pallid blue eyes. The thin, narrow-chested body below.

'You again, Peter? But this place, I'd no idea . . . So the Golden Goose has suddenly become Corrigan property?'

'As from last Monday, Mr French. We're thinking of expanding, you know. Some very nice business opportunities in Norchester, as it turns out. In and around. The way some of the restaurants here are run . . . Well, I ask you.'

'I trust, my son, any that get taken over will still be kept on strictly kosher lines. Them and the clubs. Yes, Peter? Or no?'

'But of course, Mr French. Strictly strictly kosher. Except for the food – if you get my meaning.'

'I'm glad to hear it.'

'But can I offer you something to round the evening off? A brandy? A liqueur for madame? I didn't catch your name, my dear, I'm sorry.'

'It's—'

'That's quite enough of that. I'll have the bill, please. And for every item we've ordered.'

'Of course, Mr French. Would I try to embarrass a senior officer?'

19

'If he was stupid enough to let you, yes. And now, sweetheart, why don't you go and powder your nose?'

'But, Ned, I—'

'Just vanish, darling. Yes?'


'Well now, Peter, a word in your shell-like.'

'But . . . Well, no offence, Mr French, but should I be seen talking to you? In public, as it were?'

'Yes, you creep, you bloody well should. Restaurant manager asking customer if *all was satisfactory, sir.* Can't be any harm in that.'

'If you say so.'

'I do, my son. Now, taking over this place, it means your esteemed bosses going to set up full-time in Norchester?'

Quick flashy glint in the pale eyes in the pale face.

'Why shouldn't they? Business gentlemen who—'

He over-rode the sudden touch of truculence.

'I'll tell you why they shouldn't. Because Norchester, up to now, has been a nice, law-abiding place, give or take a few rag-tag villains. But somehow I get the feeling, if only from your cocky manner, that Marty and Barty have something a good deal bigger in mind than taking over a few restaurants. So you tell me just what that is. Now.'

'But— But, no, Mr French. No, I couldn't . . .'

'Now, I said. Unless you want word to get back, say, to Farty that you've been talking to me.'

'Mr French, you wouldn't do that? You know Farty. He'd go ruddy berserk.'

'Yes, he would, wouldn't he? And when Farty gets cross people get hurt, don't they? Very badly hurt usually. So . . .'

'Oh God, Mr French, you're a hard man.'

'I am. Now, before the young lady comes back from where I sent her, give.'

'There's nothing to tell, Mr French. I swear there's nothing.'

20

'And when little Peter swears to something it means he's telling one great fat bleeding lie. So ...?'

'No. No, I can't.'

'Not even if somehow Farty gets to know what a filthy little creep you are.'

'Mr French ...'

'Now.'

'Listen, if they thought I was telling you even a whisper of this they'd crucify me. Crucify me. But— But we've always been friends, Mr French. Friends, yes?'

'Oh, yes, Peter. Bosom pals. So, just what is it they've got in mind?'

'There's ...'

'Come on, come on. The young lady'll be back in a minute.'

'Well, it's big, what they moved up here for. Really big. Too bloody big altogether, if you ask me.'

'Well, what? What? If you want to slide from under, Peter, now's your chance. If your bosses are going to go for broke over something more than they know how to take on, then you'd better tell me everything. Or you'll find yourself going down with them.'

'That's what I'm afraid of, Mr French. Dead afraid of, if you want to know.'

'All right, you're running scared. But you'll be in the shit a sight deeper if you don't have me on your side. Won't you now?'

'But, listen, Mr French, you'll be careful? There's two can play at the game you're asking me to. And you know Marty. First thing he'll do is pick up someone inside your lot. Feed him out the info. He'll work and work at that. He's clever that way. You know he is.'

'All right, so he's clever. But you'll be safe with me, Peter. Have I ever let you down? Everything strictly between you and me, till the time comes to close your friends down. Once and for all.'

'Promise, Mr French?'

'Word of honour, my son.'

'Jesus, why am I doing this?'

'Because you've gone too far now, my lad. So, the full story, and quick.'

'I can't give you the lot, Mr French. I don't get to hear all the fine print. But— But, well, it's drugs. But it's more than just getting hold of some of the stuff from down Colombia way. One hell of a lot more.'

'Tell, damn you. Tell.'

'It was Marty, Mr French. Clever-as-you-like Marty. He got to hear about this somehow. Months ago down the Smoke. There's some people opening up a new route. Who I don't know. Marty's playing this one very, very close to the chest. But some time, some time fairly soon now from what I've heard, there's going to be a bloody huge consignment coming in. To Norchester airport, where they think the Customs aren't too bright. So they're sending a load worth millions, before anybody catches on. Worth real millions on the street. It's meant to be going on from here to the continent. By what you might call the back entrance.'

'And Marty's bought his way into a share in this? Flying a bit high, isn't he?'

'No, no, Mr French. It's not that at all. Would they have the money? Would they have the clout? No, Marty's aiming to—'

A glance back from side to side. Tongue licking at lips.

'To hijack the whole lot, Mr French, up here. Where it's not being looked after too well.'

'Jesus. And he thinks he'll get away with it? That whoever owns the stuff, the Mafia, whoever, they'll just say *All yours, pal* and leave him to it?'

'But that's what he does think, Mr French. More or less. Or he reckons he'll soon make so much use of what he gets hold of no one'll be able to touch him. But I—'

'Yeah, yeah. All right, Peter, you told Marty straight out he was being stupid and he thanked you for your advice but said he was going to do it his way. Right?'

'Well, no, Mr French, no. Talk to him and Barty like that, and he'd give the nod to Farty straight away. You know that. And— And, besides, they might get away with it, you know. Be able to keep the really big boys off and make a fortune. They just might.'

'And that's something we wouldn't at all like. So just don't make the mistake, Peter my old friend, of trying to play both sides against the middle.'

'Would I, Mr French?'

'You would, Peter. So, let's hear some more. And quick.'

'Yes, Mr French. I'll tell you all I know, always will. Strike me dead if I don't. But I can't tell you more than what I do know, can I? And I've told you that. All of it.'

'No, Peter. I need to know a hell of a lot more. Just when's this stuff coming in? It'll be under some sort of cover. So what's it coming in as? What have I got to be looking out for up at the airport? This is no good to me unless I know that. For a start.'

'I can't tell you anything more, Mr French. Honest. I don't think Marty himself knows any definite date, let alone what the load's going to be coming as. Not as of now. Not judging by the way he's not doing nothing about it. Like bringing in some proper fire-power. The boys he's getting hold of up here are only good for a bit of muscle in the clubs and that.'

'Well, you could be right. Okay. But you'll keep in touch, yes? As soon as you get as much as a whisper. Of anything. Anything more.'

'Stand by me, Mr—'

'Ah, there you are, sweetheart. I've just been telling Mr Kitson, the manager here, what a good meal we've had, haven't I, Peter?'

'You have, Mr French, you have. Delighted to receive the compliment. From such a gentleman as yourself.'

\*

23

'Yes, Shirley?'

'There's a lady on the line. From the Meadows Law Centre in Nottingham. A Ms Deborah Brooke. She's asking to speak to you. On a personal matter.'

'Um. She give you any idea what personal matter it was?'

'Not really, no. She just said— Well, she did say she was representing a Ms Heather Jonas. That's the lady the *Justice Watch* programme's going to be about, isn't it?'

'It is. So *Not available*, Shirley. Just tell her that. Any time she rings.'

'Peter, fancy meeting you.'

'Mr French, how did you—'

Plain fright, fear even, in the pale face at the edge of the light still pouring brazenly from the Golden Goose's frontage.

'Perhaps I just waited here, in this nice dark corner, till you finished your evening's labours.'

'Well, yes. Yes, 'spose you did. But— But, Mr French, I don't like it. I don't like it at all. Suppose Marty'd been out here. He comes sometimes, you know, likes to sample the menu. Him and Barty.'

'And you know what I'd have done then? I'd have shaken them by the hand, said I was just waiting for you so's you could tell me what they were up to. Don't be more of a gutless fool than you can help, Peter.'

'All right, all right. But you don't know what Farty'd do to me if they ever got to know who I sometimes talk to. He'd damn near kill me. He would.'

'He'd probably make a hundred per cent job of it, my son. But I'm not going to let them hear about our little chats, am I? Not for the time being, anyway.'

'Mr French, I wish you wouldn't ...'

'And I wish you would, Peter. I wish you'd bloody keep in touch when I ask you. I haven't heard a dicky-bird from you since we talked.'

'But there's been nothing to keep in touch about, Mr French. Honest to God. I swear it. This is big, you know. Bigger than anything they've even had a smell of before. Marty's not going to spoil it, asking questions down London way. I'll let you know the moment I get to hear the least thing. I promise. Promise.'

'Well, see you do. Or . . .'

'Yes, Mr French. Yes, I will. I will.'


'It's that Ms Deborah Brooke again. She says she must speak to you.'

'Shirley, I said tell her to just go away.'

'But she doesn't. She rang three or four times last week. I don't know what to say to her any more.'

'Simple, Shirley. Just two words. Go away.'

'But she won't. And . . .'

'What *and*?'

'Well, now she says to tell you she— Well, this is what she said. She said she'd got reason to believe you were the one who really conducted Heather Jonas's interrogation.'

'Then you can tell her I wasn't. Yes? And you can add that she'd better be very careful who she goes spreading rumours about.'

'Well, I'll try.'

'Do better than that, my girl. Pass on the message.'


His private line rang. As soon as he picked the phone up and gave his name he realized from the gulping sound he heard who was there.

'Peter, it's you?'

'Yes, Mr French. Yes. And listen, just a whisper but you're going to like it.'

'Then be careful, my son. This line's no more secure than others.'

'Yes, Mr French. But— Well, let me put it like this: someone we both know's gone down to London today.

25

To— To— Well, see about hiring some staff, shall I say? Staff who— Who—'

'Who what? Spit it out.'

'Well, who'll come bringing— Bringing some ironwork. Yes, ironwork that Mar— That's wanted. For— Well, you know, for that job I mentioned.'

'That's a better boy now. You got a name? Names? Anything more?'

'No, Mr French. No. You're getting all I know. Honest. Honest.'

'Then keep in touch, my son. Keep in touch.'

'It's— Well, it's that Ms Brooke again.'

'Listen, Shirley, I've told you once and I've told you for ever. Not at home. Get that into her damned head, will you? I am not seeing her. Not on any account.'

'But— Well, what she says is it'll be worse for you if you don't. That's what she actually said. And she wants to come up here. At your convenience. She used those words: at your convenience.'

'Then tell her it's inconvenient.'

'Well, I'll try.'

'No, don't just try. Do it. That's what a secretary's for.'

'Yeah? I thought it was for something quite different.'

'That's enough. Now, go and tell that bloody woman to fuck off out of my life. For ever.'

But he flicked off the intercom thoughtfully enough.

Perhaps some counter-measures?

'Well, Graham, this is nice. Just like the old days.'

Detective Chief Inspector Graham Vaughan. Once a Nottingham detective sergeant. Ruddier in the face now. Hair of head and neatly trimmed moustache plainly grey. Heavyish body still exuding unfussed reliability.

'You in Nottingham, Ned. It's been years.'

'Yeah. Well, bit of business I had to clear up. Post-divorce nonsense. You know the way solicitors keep

26

finding things to make a penny or two more out of. Anyhow, it's given me the chance to stand you a spot of dinner, chat about old times. Pity your Margaret couldn't come along. You two still together?'

'You didn't actually invite her, Ned. But, yes, we are together. Going our own ways, but together. The way I like it, really. Live and let live.'

'Or, in your case love and let love.'

He grinned.

'Yeah, you could say that. Saves a lot of hassle. You'd still be with Myrtle if you'd been of my way of thinking.'

'Well, I'm not. You know, don't you, tolerance is not always a virtue. In fact, in my book it's often a bloody crime.'

'Same old Ned. Ever think intolerance is a crime?'

'Not often, no. Specially when I'm the one being bloody intolerant. And that reminds me . . .'

'Oh, ho. Someone in your intolerant sights, is it? Can't still be anyone down here. I'm about the only bloke left from the old days. Or me and Palmy Palmer.'

'He's still around, is he?'

'Oh, yes. And still the same as ever. Detective sergeant, and lucky to have clung to that. But I reckon the glory of that Wildfire case of yours still lingers on. Did you a lot of good certainly.'

'Oh, yes. I'm well aware what a piece of luck it was, that woman happening to fall to me and Palmy when she did.'

'Still, you've built on your luck, Ned. Well built, from all I hear. But what was it all the talk of tolerant and intolerant reminded you of? Out with it.'

'Oh, just a small thing, really. To do with the Wildfire for Wildlife case, as a matter of fact. Tell me, do you know a lady by the name of Deborah Brooke? Law Centre solicitor or something.'

'I'll say I know her. We all do. Bloody thorn in every-

27

body's side. One of those women who think every copper's worse than any villain. Always coming round. Yack, yack, yack. *You've no right . . . My client never . . .* Talk about intolerant. There's someone who'd make even you look easy-going.'

'Oh, yeah.'

'So what about her?'

'Oh, it's just that she's been on the phone trying to get to see me. On and on. It's about the Wildfire business, of course. You know some crazy sod went and confessed to planting that bomb and then committed suicide?'

'Of course. Big talking-point here, for a day or two. Nothing in it, I take it.'

'Not a thing. But this woman, Deborah whatsit, there any way I can stop her bugging me? I could do without the aggro.'

'What, you mean *Anything to her disadvantage*? 'Fraid not. We've looked about for that, the aggro she gives us. But, say what you like, the lady's pure as snow. Spends every waking minute trouncing on about her cases. Doesn't even do cannabis. Doesn't even park on a double yellow.'

'Oh, well. Let's hope she gets tired of me stonewalling. Now, tell me, how are things . . .'

# 4

'George, come in. I was just about to give you a bell.'

'Oh, yes?'

Look of slow-growing suspicion all over the solid, weather-roughened, beard-shadowed face.

'Chief's just been on to me. In a bit of a taking.'

'Is he?'

'Yeah. Seems his next-door neighbour's house was done last night. Back window job. Old housekeeper left tied up for a bit. All the loose change about the place taken. Plus the video. Say anything to you? Chief thinks it will.'

A grin.

'Loud and clear it says it. Daddy Duffell, the old rogue. His MO down to the last half-tied knot round the old lady's wrists. No harm done to her, I bet.'

'You're quite right. She wriggled loose in half an hour, but only got round to reporting it this morning. God knows why.'

'You do get 'em, don't you? However, we can't let old Daddy get away with this one. Next-door house to the Chief's. I don't suppose Daddy had the least idea, but we'll have to put him away. The lads'll pick him up in a day or two.'

'Fine, George. Just make one of your little notes.'

Abrupt reddening of muted resentment.

'Laugh at me if you like. But, let me tell you, I've never forgotten to do anything once I've been told.

29

Never. And there's not many who can say that.'

'Laugh at you, George? Would I ever?'

Nevertheless envelope and pencil stub came out from the side pocket of the creased suit. Scribble, scribble.

Then the look up. With a plain glint of malice.

'See *Justice Watch* last night?'

Quick to retaliate, old George.

'*Justice Watch*? Didn't know you went in for such things, George. Smart-alec documentary makers from the South.'

'All right, all right. I don't generally give a pig's ear for that sort of stuff. But I thought I'd see what it was all about last night. Since your name was likely to come up.'

'My name? Why should you think that?'

'You were the one who got that woman to confess, weren't you?'

'I was involved in the case, yes.'

'Well involved, from what I hear. Even if in the end *Justice Watch* didn't point out one of the officers who handled that case shot up to be Assistant Chief Constable (Operations) in Norchester. But I knew. When that story first came out you shouldn't have sent your secretary to get her *Northern Journal* back from my fancy daughter-in-law. Not if you wanted your part in it kept quiet.'

'But I didn't send Shirley to do anything of the sort. Why should I have done?'

'Well, she must have asked for the paper back on her own account then. Something you said to her? You're pretty close to that piece of goods, from what I hear.'

'Well, George, I wouldn't be the first man to be close, as you put it, to his secretary.'

'I dare say. Not that it being common practice makes that sort of thing any more right. In my book.'

'Yes. But we read different books, don't we? Still, I'm flattered you take so much interest in my early career.'

'Oh, you're not the only one with contacts in other

30

forces, Ned. I may have spent all my life in Norchester, but that doesn't mean I haven't been on a Bramshill course in my time. Made some good friends over a pint or two there. Even if we were supping southern ale. So I know just how involved, as you put it, you were in that Wildfire for Wildlife interrogation.'

'Well, yes, George, your information's spot-on. I did sit in on the interview when Heather Jonas confessed. But I hadn't been in the CID very long then, you know. Most of the questioning was done by the DS I was with.'

'Yes, my mate told me about him too. A certain DS Palmer. Still a sergeant in Nottingham when I heard about it. But you, Ned, you're no longer a detective constable, nor even a DS. You've shot up the tree. Deservedly, too. Don't get me wrong. But I think I know what put a rocket under you in the first place.'

'Well, we've all of us had a bit of luck in our careers, those of us who didn't stick at sergeant. A bit of luck, or a lot of persistence. Or both.'

'And I'd prefer persistence. Luck can go either way, you know. Sometimes, when all seems set fair, a piece of ill luck can come along, and it's down in the mire again.'

'If you call without an appointment, Miss – er – Brooke, you can't expect me to give you very much of my time. Even if you have come all the way from Nottingham to Norchester.'

Ned looked at her.

Much as he had imagined. Young. Early thirties, or a bit less. Feminine. Very, actually. Despite the big, round glasses. Or because of them. Pink-and-white complexion, abundant fall of hair. Bit tangled, of course. This sort never liked to be seen taking too much care. Same going for the clothes. Shirt with flower pattern but nary a frill, buttoned to neck. Suede jacket, bit dirt-engrained at the cuffs.

'Well, Mr French, since you haven't been available on

31

the phone ever since I've been trying to speak with you I didn't really have any alternative, did I?'

'Is what you want to see me about so urgent then?'

'Yes, it is. And don't, please, pretend you don't know very well what it is.'

A short silence.

'Right then. I do know. The Wildfire for Wildlife case.'

'I prefer to call it the Heather Jonas case, Mr French. The case of a woman serving twenty years for a crime she never committed.'

'A crime she confessed to committing, Miss Brooke.'

'Ms, if you don't mind. I can't see that my marital state is any concern of yours or anybody else's.'

'All right. Mssss. If you insist.'

'I do. And as to Heather's so-called confession, we all know nowadays how such confessions are obtained.'

'And how is that? I noticed that *Justice Watch* programme the other week wasn't exactly specific.'

'No. They had to go on air sooner than they'd have liked, so they tell me.'

'Ah. So that was the reason they did little more than produce the same old mish-mash of half-facts and second-hand reports of someone else's confession – someone conveniently dead – plus a lot of arrant speculation. The whole made to look urgent by putting their so-called witnesses in front of bits of irrelevant scenery.'

'Well, perhaps the programme wasn't as good as it should have been. Because certainly there's a lot more about Heather's interrogation which could come out.'

'Is there indeed? And what would that be? Precisely?'

'Details of the brutality employed, Mr French. Brutality, intimidation and psychological pressure of the worst sort.'

'I did ask what precisely you claim as happening.'

'Oh, don't try to wriggle out of it that way. Of course, I don't know all the exact details. Yet. For one thing it's getting on for fifteen years since you interrogated poor

32

Heather. She can't be expected to remember everything.'

'No? But if the interrogation was quite as brutal as you seem to think, Miss— Sorry, Ms Brooke, I'm surprised she doesn't recall it. In full colour.'

'She recalls some of it. Precisely. To use your word.'

'I see. But at the time of her trial, not so long afterwards, she had forgotten whatever this mistreatment was? So she never came out with it? She could have done, you know, even though she pleaded Guilty.'

'As a matter of fact the lawyers representing her were so incompetent as to advise her not to make things worse for herself by claiming to be the victim of physical assault.'

'I see. And what you're saying is that she took their advice, despite knowing she wasn't guilty? Has it occurred to you, I wonder, that she pleaded Guilty because she damn well was guilty?'

'And has it occurred to you that, if that was so, it's very odd that someone else has now admitted that it was he who put that bomb under that car?'

'Someone no longer here to substantiate that long overdue confession. If it was a confession and not some sort of bad joke.'

'And what about the fact that Heather does say now the confession she made was forced out of her under duress? Under the nastiest forms of duress?'

'Ms Brooke, I wonder if I can persuade you that what you are alleging may not be the true state of affairs? Can I even persuade you just to think in those terms? Let me put it like this: here we have a woman who, for good reasons or bad, has committed not just the murder she intended but has been responsible for the deaths of three innocent children as well. All right, under some pressure – do you expect police interrogators not to apply any pressure of any sort? – she confesses to what she has done. Later, when she is brought to court she admits the crime. Counsel claims in mitigation she had some sort of political justification. Still, she is given a long term and serves a large proportion of it. And then, quite unexpectedly, someone, a man who has taken his own life, is reported to have confessed to the crime she committed. Would it really surprise you if she thought she had an opportunity now not to serve the rest of her time? Can you think of the situation in those terms? Possibly?'

'No way. No way. Listen, I've seen Heather Jonas. Not just once, but half a dozen times. We've had long discussions. Frank. Intimate. And I'm here to tell you that she did not, did not, put that bomb under that man Reardon Smart's car. She was not responsible for the deaths of those children.'

'But, you know, Ms Brooke, once she has convinced you of that, and then induced you to persuade enough other people to believe her, she is going to get out of prison. She is going to be seen even as some sort of heroine. She is quite likely going to be granted a large sum of money in compensation. Now, will you even consider the possibility that you're wrong?'

'And you? What about you? All right, let's assume for the moment that, at the time, you genuinely believed Heather made her confession because she had actually put that bomb there. Let's assume that no afterthoughts since have led you to wonder whether you treated her in an altogether proper way. But will you now consider that you might have been wrong? Wrong all along? That Heather confessed that night because she was sick with exhaustion? Because, even, she had been so battered at and terrorized she had come to feel it was somehow possible she had done that?'

'No, Ms Brooke. No, I won't consider that. Not for one moment.'

'Then neither will I consider what you want me to believe. To believe against all my better judgment. Why should I? When, to say the least, I've got your obstructionist attitude right in front of me. When my every attempt to interview Detective Sergeant Palmer, there with you when Heather made her so-called confession, has been met with a flat refusal?'

They sat there on either side of his desk. Glaring at each other.

Then, suddenly, he felt – there could be no doubting it – zigzagging between them a sexual charge. It was ridiculous. He had been totally unaware of putting out anything in that way himself, as he might have done with some stranger at a party, or as he did from time to time with sexy little Shirley. He had registered, yes, that Ms Brooke was a more or less desirable piece of flesh. Nice figure. Pretty face. Those pink and white cheeks, what people sometimes called 'meltingly soft'. Buttony little upturned nose. The effect enhanced – yes, definitely – by the big, round spectacles with their deceptive school-mistressy look. But all along he had been too wary of her as an actual threat on a purely intellectual level to have had any reaction to her sexually. And now, without warning, this had happened.

And not just on his part. He knew – all his past experience confirmed it – that the charge that had gone from him to her had, at the same time or immediately afterwards, passed in the other direction. For some reason, or none, Deborah Brooke had experienced a strong sexual attraction to himself.

Must be those whatsits – pheromones – buzzing through the air. Extraordinary.

She stood up.

'Well, Mr French, I don't think there's anything more I've got to put to you now. But don't think you've seen the last of me.'

'I imagine not, Ms Brooke. Though I can't see that we really have any more to say to each other.'

*

35

His private-line phone ringing.

'Mr French? Is that you?'

The easily recognized voice.

'Here.'

'That multi-storey parking place, behind the cathedral.'

'I know it.'

'Top floor. Round one o'clock?'

'I'll be there. But it better be good.'

'Stand by me, Mr French.'

He took from the car pool one of the old, faceless Ford Escorts they kept for observation use. As soon as he brought the car to a halt he saw Peter Kitson sitting at the wheel of a newish grey Astra.

At this hour the top floor of the multi-storey was almost deserted. Only a handful of other cars, empty and forlorn, were scattered in the bays. For three or four minutes, looking in his mirrors and peering round without moving too much, he checked no one was there who could be watching. Then he got out, went across and leant in at the Astra's window.

'Well?'

'There's someone come up from the Smoke now, Mr French. The fire-power Marty went to get hold of.'

'Oh, yes? And who is this?'

'I don't know, Mr French. All it was, I just caught a word Marty said to Barty. And I'm telling you straight away.'

'Oh, no. You're holding out on me.'

'No. No, honest to God, Mr French. If I knew who Marty had brought, I'd tell you, wouldn't I?'

'Not if you thought you'd benefit by letting me have your little secrets drop by drop, no.'

'Listen, Mr French, I'm risking a hell of a lot coming here at all, ain't I? I mean, if Marty was to take it into his head to follow me. Or have me followed. He's got hold of some local talent. What if he's found someone

who can keep a good tail? All right, I don't suppose
they run to that in Norchester. But you never know.'

'Oh, I think it's quite likely there's more than one
local hero capable of keeping you in their sights, Peter.'

'Well then, Mr French, would I risk any more meets
than I had to? Just to keep you hungry?'

'So you've no idea who it is Marty's brought up here?
No idea at all? It is only one, is it?'

'That I do know, Mr French. Just the one. Though
from the way Marty talked about him, I'd say he's a
class act. And if I get to know a name, I'll tell you.
Right away. You can trust me for that.'

'I can't trust you for anything, Peter. Except maybe
to go peeking in public lavatories.'

'Now, now, Mr French. That ain't fair. You know I
gave up all that sort of thing long, long ago.'

'I know you told me you had, Peter. But that doesn't
mean I've got to believe you.'

'You're a hard sod, Mr French.'

'Yes, I am. And you watch out who you're putting
rude names to, or I may get rather irritated. Yes?'

'Sorry, Mr French. Sorry. Just sort of slipped out.'

'All right. But see that something else just sort of slips
out, Peter. The name of this visitor from the Smoke. A
bell. Just as soon as you hear anything. About him, or
anything else.'

'Yes, Mr French. Of course, Mr French. You can rely
on me.'

He contented himself with one last sharp glance
through the Astra's window.


'George, I've got news for you. A new face in town, and
a nasty one.'

George Grundy looked up from his desk.

'What? You mean, some London criminal? You sure?
I've not heard anything. And I do keep an eye open,
you know.'

'Yes. Well, this is via my own private line from the Corrigans. Almost bound to make me the first to know.'

A scribbled note.

'But what's this leading up to? Is that something else you know?'

'Well, yes. I have been keeping it under my hat, to tell you the truth. I wasn't at all sure at first I'd been fed anything worth having. But what I've just learnt makes it more or less certain the business is coming off.'

'Arrival of this new face of yours?'

'Exactly.'

'Right, we wondered where you'd gone when you suddenly upped and took that old Ford from the pool.'

'Listen, George, isn't it time you grew out of playing detectives on your own patch?'

'I see nothing wrong with wanting to know what's happening, when it's my business after all.'

'You ought to have a bit more trust. Even if you don't see eye to eye with someone when it comes to taking young women to bed, you ought to give them the benefit of the doubt on matters concerned with the job.'

'Well, I happen to believe you can't separate one from the other. But I'll say I'm sorry about the Ford.'

'And won't do it again?'

'I'm damned if I'll make promises.'

'All right. At least we understand one another. Which is just as well. If this business turns out to be as big as I think it is, there won't be room for any crossed lines.'

'Just how big then?'

'Oh, I'm not giving you any London bullshit, believe you me. Our friends the Corrigans have got their nasty fingers into a hell of a large pie. A sight too big for them in fact. But, if they do get to pull it off, your dear old Norchester's going to go sliding right down into the slime and most of Northern England with it.'

'I'd like to see them—'

'No. This is going to need very careful handling.

38

There's to be no rushing in wrecking everything.'

'All right. So what's the strength? Are you going to tell me or not?'

'Oh, yes. This is going to take all the resources we've got before we're done. It's like this. Marty Corrigan somehow got to know, months ago in London, that some big Colombian outfit's planning to use Norchester airport to bring in an enormous load of cocaine. Large enough to make any criminal a millionaire several times over. And the Corrigans – well, I suppose Farty's been told nothing – are planning to hijack it all before it gets moved on to the continent.'

'Hijack it? But if we know this huge consignment of Class A drugs is coming to the airport, why can't we just get in there first? Get the rotten stuff in the incinerators before it goes on to the streets.'

'I'll tell you why, George. Because I'm planning to catch the Corrigans fair and square in the act. So we not only stop that load of shit getting on to Norchester's streets and all the others, but we put the Corrigans behind bars for twenty years or more, leaving this city something like the nice place you knew when you were a kid.'

'A sight nicer then than it is today.'

'Well, a hundred times nicer than if the Corrigans get hold of the stuff coming into the airport some time soon.'

'Soon? You don't know when then?'

'No, I don't, George. I don't know when, and I don't know what it's coming in as. And unless I can drive one of our old cars out of the garage here with nobody knowing where I'm going, the chances are we'll none of us know any of that till it's all too late.'

'Are you saying security's buggered here at HQ? Let me tell you—'

'No, George. I'm not saying I know of any leaks as such. How could I when I've hardly been here twelve months? But leaks always may occur. You must know

39

that. You can't write a guarantee for everyone in this building, coppers, clerks, messengers, secretaries. You can't know for a certainty there's no one who hasn't got some weak point a clever operator like Marty Corrigan can exploit. In fact, my snout's warned me Marty's hard at work at this moment looking for an in.'

'All right. You're the boss. But I'll wager things like that don't happen in the Norchester force, not the way they do in London.'

'I hope you're right, George. It'd be the last thing any of us would want.'

'True enough.'

'Right. So, first of all I want you to make sure none of our lads with gun tickets are due for any leave. We're going to need every one of them. And before much longer.'

Another scribbled note.

'Oh, and George, one other thing.'

'Yes?'

'The Chief. No need for him to be put in the picture yet. You know what he's like. Hoping for a Sir to stick in front of the Arnold before he's done. He won't be too keen on having a gunfight anywhere on his territory. Fearfully bad publicity, even if it all comes out our way in the end. And I mean to see that's just what it does. I'm going to teach the Corrigans they can't come up here and do just what they want. Okay?'

'Okay.'

# 5

'I said we'd be seeing each other again, Mr French.'

The steady, unblinking look from behind the big schoolmistress glasses.

'And I said, if I remember, that there could hardly be anything to justify you coming all the way from Nottingham.'

'But there is. Or I certainly think so.'

'Well?'

It was still there. The to-and-fro zing of sexual attraction between them. Palpable, almost as if there was an actual substance, if not one visible to the naked eye, running in a wide conduit from one to the other, alive with crossing, intertwining currents. It had flashed into being again the moment she had taken her seat on the chair in front of the desk.

'I've got the trial transcript. At last. You'd think there was some deliberate obstructionism going on.'

'No doubt you do think so.'

'Well, wouldn't you, if it was a question of overturning a verdict the powers-that-be have been happy with for fifteen years? And if it had taken more than a month to provide the short transcript of a trial where there was a Guilty plea? Little more than the prosecution summary of the affair?'

'I wouldn't be so filled with suspicions of everyone and everything official, Ms Brooke.'

'No? I thought a successful detective would be suspicious of anything he was told.'

'Well, perhaps I am. And perhaps I shall look on what you've come all the way here to tell me with just such a suspicious eye.'

'I don't doubt my information will stand up to any amount of scrutiny.'

'So, let's hear it. I don't want to keep you longer than necessary. I suppose you've got a train to catch. Or did you drive up?'

'No, I took the train. I'll catch the 6.48 back. I go by rail when I can. You can get a lot of work done on a train.'

'Indefatigable Ms Brooke.'

'I don't suppose I'm any more *indefatigable* than yourself. Though I don't spend my time securing confessions to crimes that have never taken place.'

'Oh, come. My record, you know, is perfectly clean. Never challenged, I'm proud to say.'

'Including your conduct over poor Heather Jonas?'

'Well, I like to think her case was no different from the hundreds of others I've been involved in during my years as a detective. A great many of them resulting in convictions, I'm happy to say.'

'So you see yourself as a good detective?'

'As a matter of fact, I do.'

'Right then, how do you account for this? In Heather's so-called confession, as given in summary in the transcript, she is made to say she drove with the bomb from the camp Wildfire for Wildlife had at the site of the last Ison's Kingfishers ever to be seen in this country. She drove, the transcript says, from there into Nottingham itself, to Reardon Smart's house in The Park. But Heather Jonas had never learnt to drive, Mr French. Never. Now, what answer do you have to that?'

Did Heather say she had driven to The Park with the bomb? She had been so confused, tumbling out one thing after another in no connected order and going

42

back and back to shouting out that, yes, she had killed Reardon Smart, it had been almost impossible to sort out exactly what she had done that afternoon.

Nor had Palmy's shot-out questions been models of clarity.

'So you got this bomb, where from?'

'Where from? Where from? I don't know.'

'Come on, if you took it to put under Reardon Smart's Rolls— Rover, whatever, you must know where it was in the first place.'

'In the camp. In the camp. Does it matter? I took it, didn't I? I took it and killed that swine with it.'

'Yes, yes, you've told us that. But we've got to have the details, you know. Some details, anyhow. Now, you took the bomb and you drove down to The Park, yes?'

'I put the bomb there, didn't I? Why do you go on and on about it? I've told you. Told you what you want to know.'

He had intervened himself then.

'Listen, we have to be able to say in your statement exactly what happened. For your own good. Now, you're not from Nottingham, are you? So how did you know where to go with the bomb?'

'I knew, didn't I? I must have done if I was there. We all knew. Someone had found out where that bastard lived. We were going to picket the house. He deserved it. Self-satisfied swine. Thinking only of how much he was going to make, building all over that little wood and the stream. Concrete. Roads. Houses. Have you ever seen an Ison's Kingfisher? The most beautiful thing on God's earth, and he killed them. Killed them all. He deserved to bloody well die. I tell you that: he deserved to bloody well be blown to kingdom come.'

It had gone on and on. Eventually he had become totally exasperated. And bone-tired. Once that moment had come, the moment she had said that it had been her who had planted the bomb, a reaction had set in. Up till

43

then the adrenalin had pumped and pumped, and he had felt as fresh as if he had only just begun his day. But from then on energy had drained away. All he had wanted was to finish with the business. Get the statement, hurry to a phone, tell them at HQ they had found the bomber. The Wildfire for Wildlife bomber.

So the point had come – he had a two-seconds vision of himself at that pale cigarettes-scorched plastic table all those years ago – when he had slapped down the big pile of interview sheets, pulled out a ballpoint, poised it.

'Okay, you've told us enough. Let me just get on paper what you've said. You initial each page, sign the whole and we'll call it a day.'

He had scribbled away. His brain must have needed flogging over every line. But he had got down the gist of it. Especially those words, *Reardon Smart deserved to die. I killed him. Yes, me. It was me.* They were there in his head. Engraved. He had got them down exactly.

And, damn it, they were what mattered. Her confession. If the other details were a bit mixed up – more than a bit, probably – did it matter?

'Well, what answer do you have, Mr French? I've given you something to think about, haven't I? Don't tell me I've actually got through that impermeable police hide. Don't tell me you agree now Heather never put that bomb under that car.'

'Well, no. No, I'm sorry, Ms Brooke, I'm not going to burst into tears all over my desk and say, *Oh, you're right. You were right all along. I'm wrong. Everything I've ever believed about Heather Jonas is as wrong as wrong can be.*'

He looked at her. Expression stiffly unyielding behind the big round glasses half-way down her little button nose.

And that to-and-fro tingling still going on, back and forth, back and forth, despite the antagonism she was showing so clearly. Despite the exasperated contempt he felt for her.

'But I'll go so far as to say this: what you've told me does make me just a little uneasy. I think in fact it's very possible that Detective Sergeant Palmer, the man who's consistently refused to talk to you – perhaps wisely from his point of view – did unthinkingly speak of Heather Jonas getting from that camp to Reardon Smart's house by car. And that he spoke of it before she had said this was how she went there. It would hardly have occurred to him she would go by any other means, carrying a bomb. But, as far as I can remember, Heather accepted, perhaps even confirmed, that this was what had happened. So when I wrote out her statement – and, yes, I was the one who did that – I simply put down that she had driven to The Park. And, you know, she read over the statement before signing it. I can remember, as a matter of fact, that Palmy – that Detective Sergeant Palmer wanted to skip all that, and I insisted we should follow procedure exactly. So she read what I had written out— You know, of course, that there were no recordings of interviews in those days?'

'Yes, yes.'

'So I made sure she had seen each page before I got her to initial it, and then at the end she signed the whole as a true and correct record. A confession admitting, in plain words, that she had planted the bomb that killed Reardon Smart and those three children.'

'Yet she didn't do it, and perhaps I'll prove that as soon as I can get to see your so-called accurate record.'

'But how do you know she didn't do it? How do you really know, Ms Brooke? You've only her word for it, plus a so-called confession produced at second-hand by a man who committed suicide. But I had Heather Jonas's word-for-word admission made to me just hours after she had gone, in her hysterical way, and done that thing. A confession never withdrawn in all the weeks before

45

her trial. Never denied in all the years she was in prison. Not until just a few weeks ago.'

'But I've seen her. I've talked with her, talked and talked. Mr French, have you any idea what it's like being in prison? You should have. You damn well should have before you go putting people there on no evidence.'

'As a matter of fact I've a very good idea what prison is like, Ms Brooke. It'd be odd if I hadn't. I've questioned dozens of criminals in prisons in my time. Men and women. Now, you're going to tell me that prison can become so stultifying that someone like Heather Jonas could go through the days in a sort of shell of nothingness and—'

'Yes. Yes, I am going to tell you that. Fifteen years in prison has driven Heather to the point of having to be taken to the infirmary. Thanks to you.'

He let that jibe go by in silence. But after a moment or two, quite abruptly, he spoke again.

'Listen, do you have to go back to Nottingham on that train, the six-whatever? Couldn't you stay on a bit and come out and have dinner somewhere?'

She had accepted. It could not have been because she might hope in a friendlier atmosphere to change his mind. Or even to learn from him more than she wanted to know. He had not given the least sign that any of her arguments had convinced him. The sole concession he had made, in admitting to a feeling of unease over the discrepancy about Heather and the car, had passed almost unnoticed. And, certainly, she was not going to give in to him. It was quite plain she was by no means ready to seal a treaty of peace over a friendly meal. Nothing he had said had shaken her belief in Heather Jonas's innocence. There could be no doubting that.

So, it could only be . . .

*

46

'Shirley. Ah, you're waiting. Um. Listen, love, something's come up. I'll have to cancel. Sorry.'

'All right.'

Deborah Brooke seemed not to have noticed the mutinous look.

And, driving out, a yet more tactless piece of behaviour.

He realized, suddenly, he had turned the car into the park behind the Golden Goose. His mind elsewhere, he had blanked out on who it was who now owned the place.

Slam into reverse.

'Sorry. Not where I meant to go.'

'Why not? It looks quite nice.'

When he had got back on the road he decided to answer.

'Well, it's a question of a policeman's lot. If as a copper you happen to know that a restaurant or a club, whatever, is owned by a criminal, you don't go there. Simple as that.'

'Never off duty, is that it?'

'No, not exactly. We are allowed to have private lives, you know. It's just we have to be careful not to let the criminal world stick its dirty little paws into them.'

'Detective's work is never, never done?'

He did not respond.

What's happening to me, he was thinking. Good God, I've come to an arrangement with a fair number of women in my time. Specially since the divorce. And I think I can say I've always kept my cool. I'm sure I have. But now . . . There's that expression they have in France. *Coup de foudre*, something like that. Suppose it must exist, if the Frogs have produced a special name for it. But . . .

And something else. Niggling at the back of the mind. A woman getting out of a car back there in that ill-lit parking lot. Just ahead of us. A couple, the man already standing beside the vehicle in the dark. Familiar? Half familiar. Ringing some sort of a bell. Something not quite right? But what?

He gave it up.

'There's another place, about five miles further on. Drambleham Manor. I've not been there before, but I've heard good reports. My esteemed Chief Constable took his lady wife to it the other day. Wedding anniversary, or her birthday. Something.'

'And that's perfectly suitable for me? The awkward lady from the Law Centre? What if your Chief Constable's there again tonight? Will that be worse than you being seen with an unknown woman by some Norchester criminal?'

'Jokey jokes. I can take someone out to dinner if I want, you know. I'm a big boy— Oh hell.'

'Your car phone? Don't mind me.'

'French here.'

Three brief syllables at the far end.

'Ah, you.'

Then a request. Almost as brief.

'No, I can't. Just say what you've got to, damn you.'

Short burst of what must sound in the confined space of the car like frenzied expostulation.

'Damn you. Just give me one quick word, or I hang up.'

The quacking sound of a distant, still hurried voice.

'Yes, I know him. And it's just him? They think he's enough? They've put him somewhere, I suppose. Where?'

Whine of pleading.

'Well, find out. And find out when as well, blast you.'

The phone slammed back into its rest.

'You aren't very nice, you know, Mr French.'

'The name's Ned.'

'You aren't very nice then, Ned.'

'No? Well, in my line there's not a great deal of room for being nice.'

48

'Yes, I gathered that's what you believe. So who were you being nasty to then?'

'Can't tell you. Won't tell you.'

'As I said, not very nice.'


'Oh, come on, it's not even six yet. Still pitch dark out there.'

'And the first train goes at six-thirty.'

'But—'

'No. No, I shouldn't have stayed at all. God knows why I did. I'll be late for the office, as it is.'

'Be late. Be a lot later.'

'Tell me, are you often late in your office?'

'No. No, as a matter of fact, I never am.'

'Then . . .'

'Okay. Point taken. But one other thing . . .'

'Yes? But I must get a move on.'

'Okay. Won't keep you a moment. But, well, I seem to recall somebody saying to me not very long ago that she would be seeing me again.'

She blushed then. He could see it in the dim light of the bedside lamp.

'And you want to? Still? I may well have things to ask you. Mr French.'

'I'll risk that. And in any case I may not give you any answers. Ms Brooke.'


Not late himself at his office. If not altogether as early as usual. And George Grundy waiting for him beside Shirley's desk.

'Ned, a word if I may? Hush-hush.'

'Yes, of course. Come through. Shut the door. Sit down, sit down. Listen, I'm a bit pushed for time, but there's something to tell you. The fire-power from London. He's a fellow known as Lucy the Luger, otherwise Mario Luzzatto. Not a nice specimen. Criminal Records will fill you in. But what is it you want?'

Wait while Luzzatto's name is inscribed on a folded old letter.

Why hasn't the silly bugger learnt to write quicker than a bloody schoolchild?

'Right. Got that. But what I wanted, it's Daddy Duffell.'

'Daddy Duffell? Look, George, surely you can deal with that yourself? Or leave it to a bloody DI for Christ's sake.'

'Oh, no. This is no DI matter. Top security affair, this.'

'Come off it. Daddy, top security? April the first today, isn't it?' Eye to desk calendar. 'This some sort of an April Fool?'

'Not at all. It's just that it turns out you're not the only one with a line from the Corrigans. I've got one, too, now. Daddy.'

'But he's got no connection with the Corrigans. Come on, surely he's local as— What d'you call 'em? Norchester knobbycakes.'

'Okay, he's no smart-arse Londoner. But even the Corrigans need some local talent, and Daddy turns out to be just that. And this is the point. When we pulled him in, what should he offer us but a nice juicy something about those two, those three. In exchange for forgetting his little episode at the Chief's neighbour's place.'

'A juicy something about the Corrigans? Look, what can a petty break-in merchant like Daddy Duffell have learnt, even if they are using him for something? The Corrigans aren't little Norchester playboys, you know. They wouldn't let a fellow like Daddy know a damn thing.'

'Not just what all that Class A narcotic is coming in disguised as?'

'What? He's learnt that? Daddy Duffell's learnt how that load of cocaine's going to be labelled?'

'Just that.'

'And— And you've agreed to play ball with him? On

50

the strength of what this is he's told you?'

'I certainly have. What's a minor burglary compared to knowing exactly what to look out for at the airport when that consignment comes in? We'll know about it soon as the Corrigans. Sooner.'

'All right. So what is the consignment note going to read?'

George Grundy gave a little, tight-lipped smile and pulled an old buff envelope out of his pocket, planked it on to the desk.

On it was written, in his clumsy handwriting, two jotted words: *Stuffed Mangoes.*

'Mangoes? Mangoes? Are you telling me that stuff's coming in disguised as bloody mangoes? For God's sake, Grundy, Daddy's leading you up the bloody garden path.'

'Oh, no, he isn't. Old Daddy could never cook up a tale like that. Besides, he gave me chapter-and-verse how he got to know.'

'I'll still take a hell of a lot of convincing, even if he gave you the whole damn Bible.'

'I'll thank you not to speak of the Good Book like that. Sir.'

'Sorry. I'm sorry, George. Forgot about your beliefs. But go on. Give me old Daddy's chap— The details he told you. I'm very willing to hear.'

'Well, it seems Marty and Barty were pretty drunk when Daddy was up at their place at the South End. They were pissing themselves laughing. Talking about mangoes as if they were the funniest thing since Abbot and Costello. And in the end it came out that the mangoes were going to be fakes. Filled with the stuff.'

'I suppose it's feasible. Just. Only, damn it, I can still hardly believe it. Listen, I'm going to go and see your Daddy Duffell for myself.'

'Very well. Sir.'

# 6

On the way down to the cells, half laughing to himself about the mangoes notion, half willing to believe Daddy Duffell had somehow got hold of the truth, suddenly without any reason the thought banged into his mind. *Christ, I may not be here, see all this through.*

I could be under suspension. What Deborah said yesterday, glaring at me across the desk, why didn't it hit me at that moment? Like a swipe in the face. Why didn't it strike me all last evening, last night? Easy answer to that. Besotted, for God's sake.

But now one sentence of hers quivered electrically in his brain. *I'll prove that just as soon as I can get to see your so-called accurate record itself.*

Because that record had not been accurate. Not in one absolute essential, and one which Heather Jonas, prison stupefied as she might still be, is almost certain eventually to remember.

'Jesus, Ned, lad, look what you done here.'

'What? I got it all down, Palmy, didn't I? The guts of it anyhow.'

'Oh, yes, you got the facts of what she said. You got the most important bit all right. Exact bloody words when she said she did it. But there's one thing, lad, you totally ballsed up.'

'What, for heaven's sake?'

'The time, lad, the time. Just think how the Defence'd

make hay of you in the box if you say the interview took place at – what you put here? – 3.13 bloody a.m.?'

'Well, that's when we began, isn't it? More or less? We'll just have to let them make what they can of it. Damn it, she confessed, Palmy. There's the very words she used down here, and the whole statement's initialled by her on every page. All hundred per cent correct, right down to the word-for-word formula: *I have read the above statement and been told I can correct, alter or add anything I wish. This statement is true and I have made it of my own free will.'*

'Yeah, all right, all right. That's all fine. But, listen, lad, you don't want to give 'em a single chance, the Defence. Not if you can help it. You're new to this game, Neddy. You don't know what bloody lawyers can do to you in court when they're really trying. Twisting bastards.'

'Well, I'm sorry. But what did you expect me to do? Put down we saw her hours before we did?'

'You got it, sonny. And – yeah, look at this – I think we can climb out of the shit okay. Boxing a bit clever.'

'What then?'

'Well, first of all the date. Went and made it the ninth, didn't you, even if the ninth's scarcely begun. Trust you, clever Dick. And trust me. Don't pretend to be a brain. But I still know a trick or two. Nothing easier than to make that 9 into an 8. And the same goes for the 3 of 3.13. Just close it up and we began the interview at 8.13. Very nice.'

'At 8.13 a.m. A.m. That's going to look bloody convincing.'

'All right, we got to fix that, too. And it won't be too difficult. Look, all you got to do is put a bit of a line down the front side of that a. You write a nice round little a, lad, I'll say that for you. It'll make a lovely p, if you forget about that bit of a flick at the bottom of the a. And who's going to notice a little squiggle like that?'

'But— But, well, Sarge, don't they know, over at HQ, what time we phoned in to say we'd got her? Won't they suss out that something's wrong when they see these interview sheets?'

'Are they going to look at 'em like they're something under a microscope? Course they're not. And if they do, they know the ropes same as me. They'll keep stumm.'

As they had. If they had noticed the time at the head of the statement at all, or even if someone had spotted the alteration. But when a sharp lady like Deborah – a mental Polaroid then of a moment on the bed last night – gets to see those actual pages . . . She'll cotton on then all right. Damn it, those alterations can never have been totally convincing as a forgery. Certainly not with the a changed into a p in that pretty crude way.

And then what will happen? Deborah will press on. She wants to get that bloody woman out of gaol. So most likely it'll be a story for the newspapers, and then the Homebodies will be ringing the Chief asking for an explanation. Of something that can't be explained.

Damn, damn, damn. Why had he mocked them as Homebodies so often? In the hands of some civil servant there in Whitehall his whole career could lie in ruins. The Chief summoning him, asking for that unexplainable explanation. And whether he told the truth, or lied, or said nothing the next step inevitable. Suspension. A Police Complaints Authority investigation by some brought-in superintendent from somewhere. His report, or hers – perhaps they'll send some damn woman – going to the Crown Prosecution Service. And then . . .? Calls for a scapegoat, certainly. Probably no actual case brought against him, not after so many years had passed. But resignation? That old chestnut of 'medical grounds'? Whatever, it would mean in all likelihood he'd be well out of the building before the Corrigans descended on that huge load of disguised cocaine.

And Peter Kitson ringing and ringing and being told ACC French is 'unavailable'. Then the Corrigans making their bid – mangoes or no mangoes – and getting to be kings of Norchester, Cock of the North, eventually even Number One in London. Spreading cocaine around like it was pepper from an Italian waiter's mill.

No. Something must be done about that damn dangerous document. No matter what. Something totally bloody effective.

But, first, Daddy Duffell.

A big, red-faced, bald old fellow, worn grey cardigan just fastened across flabby chest and ponderous belly by two buttons, mismatched. Unshaven. Grey stubble. Soberly mild in outlook.

'I don't think I've had the pleasure of meeting you before, Daddy.'

'Oh. Ah. Aye, pleasure for me, just the same. If so be I knows who you be.'

Not without his mite of shrewdness, then.

'French. Assistant Chief.'

'Top o' the tree, that. Don't often get that high, not me. Not when I be in a cell. Nor when I be out, come to that. Only Mr Grundy time to time. On account o' being what they call old acquaintance.'

'Yes, and I hear you had something to tell him.'

'Oh. So I did. Ah, when you finds yourself in worse trouble than what you ever been in all your born days, you do what you can for yourself, don't you?'

'And a very shrewd move you made, Daddy. Very shrewd.'

'Ah. Yeh. What I thought meself.'

'But you wouldn't be trying to put one over on Mr Grundy, would you? I dare say you're a great deal cleverer than you let on.'

'Oh, ah, no. No, that I'm not, see. Daddy Duffell don't claim to be no master criminal. I got my ways, and I

55

sticks to 'em. Nice back window, jemmy it up, in I goes, bit of cash lying around – almost always is, somewhere – maybe a few pieces of tom on the lady's dressing-table. Then the video. I like a video. Get a few quid for a video down the pub any night o' the week.'

'Very nice. But about what you told Mr Grundy. It was just the simple truth, was it? Just what you heard the Corrigans talking about? Laughing about, was it?'

'That's it. Yes. One of 'em sort of mentioned 'em like, those what-you-call-'ems. Mangoes. And then they was off laughing. Fit to bust. And one of 'em said after a bit the best joke of all was only the top layers in them crates'd be real mangoes. Rest would all be stuffed with what was coming in.'

'And what was that, Daddy?'

'Don't know, do I? They wasn't going to talk about all that, was they, not when old Daddy were there?'

'Which one was it, Daddy?'

'Which one what?'

The bemused look. Seemed genuine.

'Which of the Corrigans first mentioned mangoes?'

'Oh, that which. Mr Grundy never asked me that. But it were that Marty. Him.'

'You're sure? You know them all well then?'

'No. No, can't say as I do. Not been in Norchester long, have they, Marty, Barty and the one what they calls Farty? And good reason for that, I can tell you. Pooh.'

'Yes, we all know about Farty. But you're sure it was Marty who let slip what he did? It doesn't sound like what I know of him.'

'Well, he was drunk like. Or a bit, anyhow. Asked me up to that big house they got. Have a few drinks. Whisky. What they call Glen-something-or-other. Right drop of stuff. And he was at it hard as the rest of us. Harder. I noticed, I did.'

'I see. And when you say the rest of us, who else was there?'

56

'Well, Barty. He was there. But not Farty, not that time. Good thing, too.'

'And who else? Or was it just the three of you?'

'No. Gismo was there, too. Only right. Seeing as how it was him who, like, introduced me to 'em.'

'Gismo? Who's he?'

'Don't you know Gismo? Thought every copper in Norchester knew Gismo.'

'Well, I haven't been here all that long. So tell me about him.'

'Well, he's Gismo, ain't he? Gismo Hawkins.'

'And why's he called Gismo? That can't be his proper name.'

'No. Course it ain't. They calls him Gismo 'cos he can do anything with a motor can Gismo.'

'I see. And what does he do for a living?'

'Well, for a living he joins up different halves of cars, all that.'

'Yes. Well, we won't go into his illegal activities just at present. But I suppose he runs some sort of legit business too?'

'Oh, ah, fair enough. Car hire. Nowadays. Had a garage once. Did stock-car racing one time. Been all sorts, so long as it's cars.'

'Right. So there were just the four of you at the Corrigans' place?'

'Yeh, that's right.'

'And the drink was flowing?'

'Oh, ah. A fair treat.'

'And why was all this? Why were you there?'

'Well, they was, like, looking me over. That's what. Know if I was a good 'un. If I could work for 'em regular. When they happened to want a little job done, like.'

'I see.'

'Told me about that place, they did. Said there'd be real good pickings, and the family off on holiday. West

Indies, bit o' sun and all that. And Marty said it was time as how I ought to be moving up to the bigger stuff. My experience.'

'This was the house you broke into? Where you tied up the old lady housekeeper?'

'Didn't do nothing that hurt her, did I? I mean, I never does. If so be there's someone on the premises unexpected, I don't hit 'em, like, do I? Just ties 'em up. So's I can get away and no trouble.'

'I'm sure you're most considerate, Daddy. It's a great credit to you. So the Corrigans told you about the house, and what then?'

'Well, nothing then. We went on drinking that stuff, that Glen-whatsit, and some time in the evening Marty mentioned that what he did.'

'The mangoes? That something was coming in at Norchester airport disguised as mangoes?'

'That's right.'

'Tell me, Daddy, what is a mango?'

'Ah, I knows that now. I caught on when they started making all them jokes. Some sort o' fruit, they are. Foreign fruit. I didn't never hear of 'em before.'

'I see. And what happened then?'

'Well, all of a sudden Marty must've thought he'd gone and said more than what he ought. Shut Barty up, he did. Smart like. Then he just mentioned the house again, the one he'd said would be a doddle and worth twice as much as what I'd ever had before. And then it all packed up. And I went home, like.'

'And nothing more was said about that cargo of stuff? Not when it was expected to arrive? Nothing like that?'

'No, no. It were just what I said. Marty clammed up about 'em. Just said about that house. Well, I reckon he never knew it was right next to who it was. But he ought to of. He really ought. You could of knocked me down with a feather when I heard. Why Mr Grundy took a special interest, I suppose.'

58

'I dare say it was. But you've got your own back on the Corrigans now, haven't you?'

'Well, I ain't going to have no more to do with 'em. Not never. I tell you that, straight. They ought to have found out the whole of it before putting me on to it, that's what. I wouldn't of gone near the place if I'd known. I mean, bound to be trouble, weren't there? Mate of your boss's, that big Chief? Good job old Gismo give me the tip after.'

'You knew about the house before we picked you up?'

'Oh, ah, course I did. Gismo got to know, see. And he told me you lot'd come and get me if you had to look for me for a twelve-month. I wanted to buzz off somewhere then. Real far away. Lie low, like. Only I couldn't think of nowhere to go. But Gismo said I could do better'n that. So I did. An' it worked a treat. It has, ain't it? Mr Grundy told me I was in the clear. Wouldn't lie to me, would he? Goes to chapel, don't he?'

'Oh, yes, Daddy, you're off the hook all right. This time. You can trot along now. If anyone asks what happened to you, say you got police bail, right?'

'Police bail. Right. Wouldn't be the first time.'

'Okay. I'll have a word with the Custody Sergeant on my way back up.'

'Well, I hand it to you, George. Way-out the idea may be, but they really seem kosher, your imitation mangoes. So I've let Daddy Duffell walk. Told him to say he got police bail, anyone asks. And, soon as my source gets me the day and the time, we'll be hundred per cent in business.'

'I'd say we are now. We've only got to find out from the airport when a cargo of mangoes is coming in from South America, and we can grab it. Get rid of the filthy stuff inside those dummies.'

'No, George. I told you: I want the Corrigans. If those mangoes were to go straight from the airport here to

59

Europe somewhere, I wouldn't be all that worried. Let the Dutch police, or the German, or the Italian sort it out. But the Corrigans aiming to hijack that load is an opportunity we won't get again. We can send those bastards down for one hell of a long time. And keep your Class A narcotics off our streets.'

'Well, I've never said I liked doing things that way. And I still don't. But you're the boss.'

'Right. But you've done bloody good work today, George. So, get the Armed Response boys put on full alert. And make sure they keep their mouths shut. You'd better go out to the airport yourself, have a discreet chat with their head of security. Take photos of the Corrigans with you. His chaps might spot one of them doing a recce, though they'd better not be told what we suspect. Okay? Oh, and I want a local called Gismo Hawkins put on the Collator list. Could turn out to be the Corrigans' driver on the day. So any sightings could be worth having.'

'Gismo Hawkins. You'll get plenty of sightings of him. Always hanging round wherever there's a bit of trouble. But they won't mean anything, I'll tell you that. Gismo's nothing but small fry. We've had him taped for years.'

'Nevertheless, George, I want him marked.'

'If you say so . . .'

Envelope out. Ballpoint picked up from the desk. Quick note.

'And the sooner you're up at the airport yourself the better. Any time now this phone may ring, and I'll have to take one of those old Fords from the car pool. Final rendezvous.'

But would he be here at Headquarters in the control room to hear the progress of the ambush when the time came? To direct it, perhaps, if things did not go to plan?

Or would he be sitting at home, under suspension, fretting? Would he even be able to make that final rendezvous with Peter Kitson? And something was niggling at him about the talk with old Daddy Duffell. God knows what. But, with that looming thought of what would happen as soon as Deborah set eyes on the forgery in Heather Jonas's statement, had he been as alert as he should have been? Giving it a hundred per cent? Shaking soft old Daddy till his bones rattled, silly old fool?

No. Something must be done about the statement. And done quickly. Or there could be no new meeting with Peter, and no way of getting to know when the Corrigans planned their raid. The whole thing could happen with no one at HQ knowing anything about it.

So, of course, it was plain what had to be done.

# 7

'Hello? Fred Palmer here.'

'Palmy. An old friend. Sorry to call you at home on a Sunday, but I happen to be here in Nottingham. Ned French.'

'Who— Ned Fre— Mr French, is it you?'

'Who else, Palmy, old friend?'

'Well, seeing as how I haven't heard a dicky-bird from you in all the years since you left here to go to the Met . . . Well, this is a surprise.'

'Yes, I suppose it must be. But I think actually we've got something to discuss.'

'Discuss? What discuss?'

'A certain interrogation we once shared. Long time ago.'

'Oh. Yeah, that Heather—'

'Enough said. Can we meet somewhere? Somewhere anyone who knows us won't see us together?'

'Yeah. Yeah, know what you mean. Now, let me think. Where would . . .?'

'I suggest that big pub down by the Trent at Wilford Bridge, if it's still there after all these years. The Toll Bridge, I think it's called. Big garden at the edge of the sports ground. Benches outside. Just right for a quiet chat.'

'Don't know it.'

'Oh, come on, Palmy. You've been in Nottingham all this time, you must know where Wilford Bridge is.'

'Jesus, I know that. It's just I don't know the boozer. Haven't been down that part for years. I'm up at Headquarters now, you know.'

'All right. But you can find it, can't you? All the better that no one in there's likely to know you.'

'All right. Good thinking, I s'pose. Six o'clock suit you?'

'I'll be there.'

Make another call? Shouldn't really. Shouldn't let the lady know I'm down in Nottingham at all. Yet . . . Well, I don't have to be in the office till nine o'clock tomorrow morning.

'Deborah? It's me, Ned. Ned French. Sorry to call you out of the blue, but I happen to be here in Nottingham. Somebody I had to see to do with my ex-wife. Divorce stuff. Come up again many years on.'

Liar.

'Oh, yes? You never said you were likely to come down here when we talked about seeing each other again.'

'Well, no. No, I didn't. I— Well, let's say that was very early in the morning and I wasn't thinking too straight. But the point is: I'm here. Now.'

'Oh, yes?'

'What d'you mean, *Oh, yes*? Can I come round a bit later, or not?'

'Yes. Yes, well, yes. Only I've got some work to do. Something fairly urgent.'

'Rescuing some criminal from the wicked hands of the police, is it?'

'Not quite like that, no. But I've got to get it done before tomorrow. When do you have to be back in Norchester?'

'That rather depends on you.'

'You mean ACC French might actually be late at his office tomorrow morning?'

63

'No, damn it, he won't be. But he could go straight to the office from the motorway.'

'He'd better do that then, hadn't he?'

'Well, Palmy, it's been a long time.'

And you, you're the same if a bit different. The same beer belly, but that much slacker. The same rheumy eyes, but the lines round them deeper. Cut deeper by, surely, an added knifing of bitterness. Same long face, bit more weatherbeaten, drink-flushed. Same old look, though, half shifty, half crafty. Same old Palmy.

'Tell you the truth, I expected it'd be a very long time. Like always. Way you went shooting up the tree like you done. ACC (Operations) now, ain't it? Up in the frozen North somewhere?'

'Norchester. Not so very far from Nottingham. Once you're on the motorway.'

'So how come, then, you don't buzz down to see old mates here, time to time? Come to that, London's even nearer than Norchester. And we didn't see you ever, once you'd gone to the Met.'

'No. Quite right. I'd got thieves to catch down there. Plus the divorce, and Myrtle being a Nottingham girl. Best not to be around, you know.'

'I dare say. But now, when something a bit nasty from the old days rears its head, all of a sudden here you are.'

'Yes. Here I am. But that business is more than a bit nasty. Believe you me.'

'Is it? I dare say it is. For an Assistant Chief. But it won't do me much harm. I finish in a few months. I'll have me pension. Be snug as a bug in a rug.'

'Okay. Maybe you will be. But how snug are you now? Really? I gather a lady from the Meadows Law Centre's been trying to interview you.'

'What if she has, the silly bitch? We know all about bloody Ms Brooke here, and I'm damned if she'll get so much as a sniff out of me.'

64

'All the same she could make trouble for you, whether you talk to her or not.'

'What trouble? I ain't done nothing wrong. Maybe I gave that Wildlife cow a bit of a hard time, but I never did nothing no one else wasn't doing in those days. Even if she wasn't guilty after all.'

'Not guilty? You believe that?'

'Well, could be, couldn't it? I mean, she was a stupid tart all along. That was plain enough. Sort who's ready to cough to something she never done at the drop of a hat. I could believe that was the way it was, no problem. I could believe it either way, of a bint like that.'

'Well, if she really was innocent . . . If that bloke who confessed to it to his friend really did plant that bomb, then you're well and truly in the shit.'

'Maybe. But even if I am, you're in it a whole lot deeper. Any inquiry could overlook what I done. I mean it was all those years ago, after all. At worst I'll just get a reprimand. Fined ten, fifteen days' pay. No skin off my nose. But an Assistant Chief, the press'll go mad to see you're done over proper.'

'I dare say they would. Which is why certain measures have got to be taken. And quickly. For your sake as well as mine. You realize that somewhere in the HQ files here in Nottingham there's a statement signed by Heather Jonas? Timed at 8.13 p.m., as I remember. When she'll know bloody well we began our interview with her in the middle of the night. Or at 3.13 a.m. to be precise.'

'God, yes. I'd forgotten that. You fixed the figures, didn't you? I'd clean forgotten.'

'And perhaps you've clean forgotten, too, whose bright idea that was?'

'You're saying it was mine? I don't remember that, no way.'

'Well, I do. And if the worst comes to the worst, I won't move one inch to cover your back. Mate.'

'Like that, is it, Mr High-and-mighty? Well, you can

stew your own damn juice then. Fucked if I care.'

'You sure? If it all comes out, you were the senior one there. You were the full DS while I'd only just made the CID. No one's going to believe I ran that whole interview on my own, whether it led to a wrong confession or not.'

'I don't see why they shouldn't. You're the one who's had the career since, ain't you? They'll see you as the sort who'd do anything to grab a bit of glory. I could step out of it, pretty well shit-free.'

'If you believe that, Palmy, my old friend, you'll believe anything. Never mind reprimand, you're in line to be dismissed the force. And then where's your nice little pension going to come from? Remember which one of us it was who really gave Heather Jonas a hard time? Hands on the table, whack down the handcuffs? Stamp on her old rubber boots? She'll remember who all right, even if you don't.'

Silence now. Pint on the table in front of him untasted.

'All right. Suppose there's maybe something in what you say. So what's the big idea you got?'

'Very simple. That statement of Heather Jonas's goes missing.'

Another silence. Beer cautiously sipped.

'Yeah. Suppose that's the only thing. You're right. So, why've you come to me?'

'Because you're going to take that statement out of the files.'

'Me? Me? Why the hell should it be me? I don't mind sussing out where the bloody thing is, if you like. But if there's going to be any lifting it, it's you what's going to do it. You're the one with most at stake.'

'I don't deny that. Not a bit. But, as it so happens, just because I'm who I am now I can't go waltzing into Nottingham Constabulary HQ and slip down to Records.'

'I don't see why not.'

'Because I'm not known in the building nowadays, am I? If I go stepping in there, right away someone's going to ask for ID. And then they'll know that Assistant Chief Constable French was there when a file, possibly incriminating him, went missing.'

'But—'

'Whereas, if DS Palmer goes wandering about in his own building, people'll just think he's skiving off from doing something he doesn't want to do.'

'Here—'

'Come on, it's true, isn't it? No one's going to ask you what you're doing among the files? If it comes to that, you've actually got a right to go looking for old information there. Not that you'd ever trouble yourself to, if what I remember of you's anything to go by.'

'You don't bother to hide your opinions, do you?'

'Well, no, I don't. I never have. You're a disgrace to the service, Palmy Palmer. You always were, and you are still. But you're a shit who's now got to do what happens to be useful to me. There's nothing else left to you, not if you want to make sure of saving your own skin.'

'Christ, you're a hard bugger.'

'What got me to where I am, Palmy. So, soon as ever you can, get hold of that statement. And, when you do, I want to see it. I don't want any cheerful word down the blower that you've burnt it. I want the evidence of my own eyes. So send it straight to me. At home. Right?'

'All right, if I must.'

'Stop. Stop.'

'No.'

'No, stop, Ned, damn you. That hurts.'

'No.'

'Oh. Oh. Oh.'

'Ah . . .'

'Christ, Ned French, you're a hard man.'

'Don't deny that. But it didn't faze you in the end, did it?'

'Well, I don't know about that.'

'Oh, yes, you do. You liked it. Admit it.'

'No, I bloody well won't admit it. That fucking well hurt me. Hurt me. All right, I didn't altogether hate it. But I didn't damn well like it either. So, remember that.'

'Well, at least you're asking me to remember your every last squeamish wish. Means you'll be happy coming back for more.'

'All right, I don't say that I won't. But my wishes are not bloody squeamish. I've got rights too, you know.'

'No. I don't.'

'Now, listen, if you're going to come the chauvinist pig this'll be all off. Don't make any mistake about that.'

'And who's coming the sodding intransigeant feminist?'

A long silence.

'Well, I am a feminist. And proud of it. I don't know about the intransigeant, though. I'm a lot less intransige-ant than you. I know that.'

'That wouldn't be difficult. Intransigeance is a good thing in my book.'

'In your detective book, maybe. But do you have to drag it into every aspect of your life?'

Short silence.

'Yes. Yes, I think I do. You once asked me if I saw myself as a good detective, and I replied, in all honesty, that I did. You seemed to accept that even. Well, if I am a good detective, what's made me one is intransigeance. Persistence. Determination to hunt down offenders. Make them pay. And you can't turn that on as you step into Police Headquarters and then turn it off when you step out.'

'All right. But, remember, I can't turn off my feeling that a woman's got rights when I step into bed with you. The feeling that every woman's got rights, and that for years and years they've been happily trampled on by men like you, Ned French.'

'We back to Heather Jonas by any chance?'

'We're never all that far away from her. Or I'm certainly not. She's a classic example of what intransigeant men like you and your friend Detective Sergeant Palmer can do to a defenceless woman.'

'Not so defenceless. The vindictive bitch killed that fellow Reardon Smart, remember. Let alone three innocent little kids along with him.'

'Only she didn't. That's where we quarrel, Assistant Chief Constable French.'

'So you still think every word that opportunistic lady chooses to tell you is gospel truth, do you?'

'And you still think that every word you and Sergeant Palmer extracted from her is untainted by any sort of fear or overwhelming pressure?'

Another silence.

'As a matter of fact, I don't. Not altogether. I suppose it has never occurred to you that I might have been thinking about that night— That evening, rather. That evening. I suppose you can't bring yourself to credit that, ever since the business came up again, I've been asking myself if I was strictly within limits when we interrogated her. If Palmy Palmer was.'

'And what answers have you come up with? You can tell me, can't you?'

'No. No, I can't. You'd use it.'

'Well, perhaps I might, yes.'

'You don't think all this—' A ringing smack. 'Will make any difference?'

'Not to me it won't.'

He looked down at her.

'But, actually, sweetheart, the time may come when it does make a difference. To me. It'll be more difficult for me to make an appeal to you, Ms Deborah Brooke, crusader. And it's possible that at some time I may need to do just that.'

'An appeal? What sort of an appeal?'

A sudden sharply appraising look.

'That'd be telling. And just at present I've no intention of telling you a thing.'

Pause for thought.

'Well, I'm glad to hear at least you see there may be a time for us beyond *just at present.*'

His pause for thought.

'Not making promises, mind. But, tell you the truth, I haven't ever got as far as thinking about promises with any other woman in all the time since my divorce.'

She looked up at him.

'Well, I'm flattered. And how long has that been?'

'What *how long*?'

'Since your divorce. You realize I didn't know till just today that you'd even once been married.'

'Suppose not. We haven't actually seen very much of each other, have we? And we've been otherwise engaged most of the time we have been together. Either wrangling over bloody Heather Jonas. Or this.'

He dived.

But before long she pushed him back, spoke again.

'So how long is it since your divorce?'

'Eh?'

'How long has it been since you were divorced, I asked.'

'Oh, that. Twelve years. Thirteen.'

'And you still have to come to Nottingham to see somebody about it?'

'See— Oh, yes, I told you that, didn't I? Well, these things are apt to go on and on, you know. One way and another. Stuff affecting the alimony, all that.'

'Your ex asking for more, now that you're a top cop?'

'Yes. Yes, that's it. And now you and I have got a bit of unfinished business. Yes?'

'Oh, yes. Yes.'

# 8

He got into his office at five to nine, almost late despite having left Deborah at a very early hour. Shirley was at her desk. She waved the telephone receiver at him.

'It's that fellow you speak to, the one who never gives his name. This early. He says he couldn't get through on the private line.'

'Right. I'll take it inside. Don't let him ring off.'

'Okay. But hurry. He sounds like a little boy wanting the toilet.'

The door behind him jerked open. George Grundy.

'George. Good morning. Be with you in a moment.'

'I only want a quick word.'

Without pausing he strode past and entered the inner office. Ned followed, giving Shirley an eyebrows-lifted glance.

'Tell him I'll be with him in just a minute. Yes?'

'Okay. But—'

He shut the door. Carefully.

'What is it, George?'

'It's Cindy. My damn daughter-in-law.'

'Oh, yes? What about her?'

'Well, it's like this. You know DI Smithers, in charge of Fingerprints?'

'Yes, yes. Of course I do. But what about him? Look, George, I've got a call waiting.'

'Okay, okay. Keep your hair on. I said I wouldn't be a minute.'

'Right. Well, what about Smithers then?'

'It's not him. It's that slut Cindy. I should never have let my Frank marry her. He's always been weak.'

'George, what is this? I don't really want to hear all your family history.'

'No, no. I'm sorry. Truth is, I don't much want to tell you. But I can't see any other way round.'

'Round what, George?'

'Cindy. That bloody girl. See, Jack Smithers tells me she's always skipping out of the Bureau when she should be working. Away as much as an hour. Day after day. He doesn't know what she's up to, but he says it's making his job impossible.'

'So why doesn't he bawl her out, for God's sake?'

A huge grampus sigh.

'He wants to. Wants to have her out of it altogether, in fact. Only, because she's my daughter-in-law he doesn't want to.'

'Well, let him make up his bloody mind one way or the other, right? Now, look—'

'So he came to me. Would I have her up, give her a talking-to?'

'All right then. Why don't you?'

'I meant to, damn it. Told the tarty bitch to come to my office. And then— Well, if you want the truth, when I saw her standing there, daring me to say anything . . . She knew what she was there for all right. Well, I ducked out. Literally, if you must know. Remembered a fake appointment.'

'Why, for heaven's sake, George? You're not afraid of a girl like that, are you?'

'No, I'm not. But I suddenly realized if I said anything she'd make even more trouble for Frank. Leads him a dog's life as it is, damn selfish miss.'

'George, what is it you want?'

'Look, I don't like having to ask, but that's what I'm doing.'

'Ask what?'

'Ask you to have that damn girl up in front of you, tell her DI Smithers has complained to you, give her the tongue-lashing she deserves.'

He looked at George.

'Okay. Yes. Right. I'll do it. Later. That's a promise. I'll let you know how it goes. Now, I'd better take that call.'

'Yes. Yes, of course, Ned. And thanks.'

Humiliated broad back retreating.

'Shirley. He still there? Put him through, for God's sake.'

Grab at phone.

'Hello.'

'Mr French, is that you?'

Thank Christ.

'Date? You got it? And the place?'

'I got something you need to know. Urgent. That spot we once fixed on, out in the country? In half an hour. Sooner.'

'Peter— Damn.'

The whine of a disconnected line.

The rendezvous was a minor crossroads on the way out to the airport as it cut through a large area of scrubbily wooded heath, the remains of the medieval Parbrook Forest. On a hill above was a dark grey obelisk. Someone had once told him it commemorated the Battle of Trafalgar. Peter Kitson's Astra was parked inside the track-like road leading to the hill in a narrow ravine, known locally as a clough. Unless you were looking you would not have known it was there.

He wound down his window as Peter came climbing up.

'Bugger you. What the hell's up with you? Do we have to meet all the way out here?'

'We do, Mr French. I'm not going to risk anywhere in Norchester. Not now.'

'What do you mean, *not now*? What's happened, for God's sake?'

A harassed look from side to side, even right out here in this bare stretch of heathland with the wind suddenly gusting.

'Come on, blast you. What's happened?'

'I'll tell you what's happened. Marty's got a line out of your place. That's all.'

'A line? He's found someone to blab? Who? By God, when I get hold of them I'll . . .'

'I don't know who, Mr French. I'd be quick enough to tell you if I did. Whoever they are they'll likely be handing me to Marty before I know where I am. And he'll give me to Farty. Like a bloody piece of fish to a cat. I'd be a goner then, wouldn't I?'

'I dare say you would. So I suppose you're going to tell me now you want to call off our arrangement. Going to say you daren't risk meeting me any more? Well, you've got another think coming, my son. Tell me how you know about Marty having a source inside. What's to stop this being a nasty little tarradiddle you've put together for my benefit?'

'Honest to God, no, Mr French. It's straight up. Straight up. I heard it from Marty himself. He told Barty while I was there in the room. He'd had a leak that you lot knew what the stuff coming in at the airport was going to be disguised as. Mangoes, he said. First I knew of it.'

'Mangoes? He said that we knew the stuff was coming in as a cargo of mangoes?'

'That was it, Mr French. True as I'm standing here.'

'All right then, Peter, I believe you. This time. But you know what it means, you being there when Marty mentioned those mangoes?'

'No, Mr French.'

'It means, my lad, that Marty hasn't got the least idea about our little arrangement. Yes? If he had, would he let you get even a hint he knows what we've found out?'

74

'Well, you could be right, Mr French. Yes, you could be right. But how long's it going to last like that? You shouldn't have put a watch on the house in the South End, Mr French. I had to do a lot of talking to persuade Barty it wasn't because of a whisper you'd had. He'd spotted one of your lot all right.'

'But I haven't— Come off it, my son. There's no watch on the house.'

'If you say so, Mr French. You ought to know. But Barty's sure there is. I tell you that.'

'Well, there isn't, Peter. Barty's got it wrong.'

'All right. But, in any case, how long's it going to be before whoever's talking to Marty among your lot'll tell him you go out in this tatty old Ford and meet up with Peter Kitson?'

'It's going to be a long, long time, Peter, my old friend. For one simple reason. Nobody, but nobody, in the whole City of Norchester Constabulary knows your name. No one from my esteemed Chief down to the newest cadet in the force. Okay? You're not even on the Informants Register. Thanks to me and a little bit of forgetting.'

'If you say so, Mr French.'

'I do, my son. So now you've got a whole lot more to find out. When that raid's going to be. Just where Marty plans it's to happen. At the airport? Somewhere on the road? Where? Plus I want the name of that mouth of Marty's. Badly. Yes?'

'It's a lot to ask, Mr French. I got to go cautious, you know.'

'I know you'd go so bloody cautious if you were let I wouldn't hear from you this side of Christmas.'

'Mr French, I'll do my best. When have I ever done anything else? For you, Mr French?'

'Whenever you thought you could get away with it, my son. But not this time, see. This time there's too much at stake.'

\*

75

But, driving back from that rendezvous under Obelisk Hill, he saw the result he was determined to get becoming more and more difficult to achieve. If Marty Corrigan had a source inside Norchester Constabulary headquarters any unavoidable early preparation for ambushing his team as they made their bid could well be signalled back. Then he could easily delay the whole operation. Or advance it. Or anything.

So who was it Marty had got his claws into? Some member of the Armed Response team? Already? Perhaps the most likely. A macho bunch. As they had to be. But because of that all the more inclined to put it about sexually. And there's a weakness. The very sort a clever, calculating sod like Marty Corrigan might get hold of.

Not that there weren't others almost as likely. Young Shirley even. He'd not taken her out since Deborah. Could be some jealousy, some spite, there. And, though he was always careful not to let her learn anything she shouldn't, the possibility couldn't be ruled out. Nor could it elsewhere. Keep information to as limited a circle as possible, still more than a handful had to know at least something. Local Intelligence office, should be as secure as anywhere. But even there someone might have some unknown weakness. One that could have come to Marty's ears. Some sudden illicit sexual peccadillo. A too large debt unexpectedly incurred. A relative in trouble. Anything.

Or there was something as simple as canteen gossip. An incautious word across a table. A bit of a boast. Anyone Marty had somehow suborned might have flapping ears for those. Canteen staff, cleaners.

Bugger, bugger, bugger.

His internal phone buzzed.

'Yes?'

'George here, Ned.'

'Look, George, I'm sorry but I haven't had a chance even to think about your Cindy.'

'Ned, it's not that stupid girl. It's some bad news. Damn bad news.'

'What? Well?'

'Daddy Duffell. The beat officer on the edge of Pratts Town, down by the old gasworks, happened to see the door of one of those derelict houses there swinging open. Went in to rout out any druggies or other scum. Found Daddy Duffell. Dead.'

The moment you entered through the swinging-open, almost paintless front door the high thin smell of layer on layer of rat droppings penetrated the nostrils. It took Ned back at once to his active days. This might be Norchester, but the odour was no different from what he had smelt in any of the grottiest parts of London in his days as a detective sergeant.

The body was in the back room.

It was plain it was Daddy Duffell. The same thin grey cardigan he had been wearing when he had questioned him in the cells at HQ was still somehow held together over his tub-of-lard belly by the same two mismatched buttons. But the face was unrecognizable. One eye no longer in its socket. A thick paste of congealed blood, crawled over by a few bloated bluebottles, hid the bald head and most of the features. Another smell fought with that of rats' droppings.

'Poor bugger,' George Grundy said.

'Amen to that.'

Ned looked round.

The peeling wallpaper was splashed in patches with blood. At one place the flimsy lath-and-plaster wall dividing back room and front looked as if it had been thrust inwards by a body being rammed into it with extraordinary force. On the narrow metal mantelpiece over the pawky little grate a pinky-grey mess, brains probably, dangled sickeningly.

He turned to the white boiler-suited Scenes-of-Crime inspector, already busy at work with his team.

'How's it going?'

'Pretty much according to Cocker, sir. The doc's been. Death's been certified. Not exactly difficult. And we've had the usual unwillingness to put a time to anything until they've had the cadaver on the slab.'

'Well, we hardly need Forensic to tell us what happened, do we? Battered to death, I should say about sums it up.'

'Yes, sir. Not a nice way to go. Poor old Daddy, he never did a quarter this much harm to a living soul. Not a tenth.'

'Well, we'll get the bugger who did it to him,' George Grundy said. 'You can be damn well sure of that.'

Ned waited till they were out on the broken pavement just beyond the house, sucking in great lungfuls of fresh, rain-damp air.

'You know who did this, George,' he said.

'If all I've heard about Farty Corrigan's true, we won't have far to look. That it?'

'Yes. His trademark. And we know old Daddy was in with that lot, and that he sold them to us.'

'Right then.'

'George, you're not going to like this.'

'Like what?'

'I don't want Farty brought in.'

# 9

George Grundy was still arguing long after they were back at Headquarters.

'With respect, sir, it's this simple. A murder's been committed. We know who committed it. Or we've a pretty good idea. It's our plain duty to have the sod in for questioning. At the very least.'

'We can't know it was Farty beyond all doubt.'

'Oh, come on. With respect, who else would have done that to poor old Daddy? And, what's more, it's plain enough why. Somehow the Corrigans found out Daddy grassed.'

'Yes, you're right. My mistake to bring in the legalities. But the truth of the matter still is it'd be disaster to interfere with the Corrigans at this time.'

'Interfere? Damn it— Sir, it's not interfering, it's seeing bloody justice done.'

'Look, you know what Marty will do if we pull Farty in?'

'I suppose you're going to say he'll drop the idea of snatching that load of Class A drugs. Well, if he does, he does. We can seize it ourselves, charge anybody involved, eventually put the stuff in the incinerators, where it bloody well belongs. And that'll be that.'

'No, you're wrong, George. Neither Marty nor Barty will give this up now. It's their one big chance to move into the premier league.'

'Well, what will they do then?'

'Our Marty will set about providing Farty with a damn good alibi. It won't be the first time he's done something of the sort down in London. He'll find two or three witnesses, with unblemished records, mind, and he'll have them swear black and blue they were there sitting round a card-table playing kalooki or whatever with Farty. At the exact time Daddy was killed.'

For almost half a minute George Grundy was silent. Lips pressed close together. Eyes bulging with suppressed fury. Then he spoke.

'Sir, I admit I had no intention of telling you this. But the fact is I've had the Corrigans' place up at the South End under obbo ever since you told me what they had in mind.'

A moment of blank incredulity.

'You fool, Grundy. You bloody stupid fool. Did you think the Corrigans are so simple they wouldn't have seen what's happening? Christ, I didn't believe it when my nark told me Barty had spotted someone. I flatly denied we were doing it.'

'I— I'm sorry, sir. If I find out who let themselves be seen, I'll—'

'Never mind that. It was you who gave whoever was spotted their orders, and now you've warned the Corrigans. You've bloody well warned them we think there's something in the wind. And if they haven't been scared off altogether, it's only because there's too much in it for them to let it all go.'

'With respect, sir, that watch at the house has already paid off. Yesterday the airport head of security rang me. Someone who fitted Marty Corrigan's description was acting suspiciously up there. Having a fair old nose around. And . . .' Balloon-like self-confidence beginning to puff back. 'And straight away my men at the house confirmed Marty had left the place. So we know something, don't we? We know Marty plans to make his bid at the airport itself.'

'All right. We're all the better for knowing that. I grant you that much. But let me tell you something else. That team on obbo out there did worse than warn the Corrigans. It put the life of my informant in danger.'

'But—'

'No, hear me out. My fellow had to talk hard to Barty to convince him the house wasn't under surveillance because of a whisper we'd had. And he's by no means sure he succeeded. Do you want him to be given to Farty like old Daddy Duffell? What the hell do you mean by giving an order against my direct instructions?'

'Sir, let me point out you had never directly ordered me not to have that house watched.'

Ned drew breath.

Perhaps in the end the Corrigans had reckoned the watch was no more than provincial rabbits showing themselves scared of big London cats coming to their patch. Perhaps. And the obbo had revealed Marty's visit to the airport. So it was clear now. The Corrigans' raid, when it came, would be on one of the airport's refrigerated transit sheds while the disguised load was waiting for the people who owned it to fix up onward transportation.

Something gained.

'Very well, we'll say no more about it. But I want those men of yours withdrawn. At once. Understood?'

'Sir. But let me point out we've gained one other advantage having them out there. If Marty Corrigan produces an alibi for Farty, we can do better. We can bring up two police officers, hundred per cent trustworthy, who were keeping that house in the South End under surveillance. They'll say in open court that Farty left it at such-and-such a time. Even that when he came back they could see blood on his clothes.'

'Which may not have been there. I hope you're not suggesting your witnesses produce more evidence than there is.'

'Well, and if they do, it'd be no more than a sub-human like Farty Corrigan deserves.'

'But I won't have it. Understand? I've never tolerated that sort of thing, and I'm not going to begin to countenance it now. Corrigans or no Corrigans.'

He came to a halt in silence then.

Never?

'So you got in a car and took that bomb down to that big house in The Park?'

In his head he could hear Palmy Palmer banging out the question, with as much vividness as if it had been shouted at Heather Jonas not all those years ago but yesterday.

'I killed Reardon Smart. I killed him. He deserved to die.'

'Then what did you do when you got to The Park? Tell us the truth. You left your car some distance away from the house. You'd got the bomb in some sort of a bag. A shopping-bag, yes?'

'Yes, yes. What does it matter what the bomb was in? It killed that swine, didn't it? And it was meant to.'

And at the end of that muddled, hysterical, contradictory session he himself had put it all into order for the statement. *I placed the bomb in a shopping-bag for the purposes of concealment. I then took one of the cars at the camp at Tottle Brook. I drove with the bomb to the house of Mr Reardon Smart at No. 34, Park Drive, The Park, Nottingham. I took the opportunity of placing the bomb with the trigger set.*

'So when did you set the trigger?' Palmy had stormed at her. 'When? Come on, when? We got to put that in your statement, you know. So come on. When was it?'

'What trigger? I don't understand. Reardon Smart wasn't shot.'

'Oh, for God's sake, woman, the trigger device that made the bomb go off when Smart got into that Rover.'

82

'I don't know. If you say I did that, I must have done, mustn't I? I killed Reardon Smart. Killed the swine. As he deserved to be. How many more times have I got to tell you that?'

He shook his head from side to side. Sharply.

'No, George, if eventually we charge Farty with Daddy Duffell's murder, if in the end we find we can, then it's going to be done one hundred per cent according to the book.'

'If you say so. I've never yet disobeyed a direct order. But I swore, there in that stinking house, I'd get the swine who did that to old Daddy, and I still think he ought to be got. Now. And by fair means or foul.'

'No. Listen. Point one: I'm letting Farty go free now, and there's no going back on that. Point two: when this business is over, when we've pulled in all three of the Corrigans as they ambush that load, then we'll stick that murder charge on Farty so there'll be no alibi-ing him out of it whatever the Corrigans' brief can say. Right?'

'By that time half the evidence will have melted away.'

'I don't think it will, necessarily. But – let me make this quite clear – even if we knew for a certainty it would, I'm still not having Farty pulled in. Nothing's going to stop me taking out the Corrigans. Like an ulcer. I'm going to rip that foulness out before they begin on all the harm they'll be able to do. But it's not going to be easy. You know that, don't you? We can't afford a single weak spot.'

'All right, it's a tricky affair, I grant. But I still don't see there are any of your weak spots.'

'Don't you? Well, let me tell you something. I was trying to make up my mind how far it should go, on a need-to-know basis, when you rang to tell me about Daddy Duffell.'

'And I wasn't going to be let know? That it?'

'I'll be frank. I'd half a mind to keep it absolutely to

myself, at least until my hand was forced. Because it's top security.'

He looked over at his door.

Tight shut.

'George, bloody Marty Corrigan has got hold of someone here inside.'

'Someone? Who? You're sure?' An abrupt change of tack. 'You got the whisper from your famous nark, I suppose. How can you be certain Marty hasn't just guessed something?'

'Oh, no. I had it loud and clear. Marty knows we know what it was exactly that Daddy Duffell told us, that the stuff's coming in disguised in a load of mangoes.'

A swallowed acceptance.

'But this nark of yours, did he give you any idea who Marty Corrigan's got hold of? I'd have sworn ...'

'Oh, think, George. Everybody's human. Offer anyone enough, get hold of anyone who's in a really damaging situation, and in the end they'll feed out whatever they can.'

'I know I bloody well wouldn't.'

'Well, I hope I wouldn't either. But that doesn't stop me realizing that there are more weak individuals in this world than there are strong. In this world, or in this headquarters come to that.'

'Suppose you're right. So what are you going to do? Put Jackson in Internal Affairs on to it?'

'I could. But, to tell you the truth, I haven't got all that high an opinion of Detective Chief Inspector Jackson. Prejudice it may be, but I don't think too much of anybody who'd leave the sharp end to go rubber-heeling through the force.'

'Know what you mean. So what's to be done?'

'Precious little, I'm afraid. Be bloody careful ourselves over everything we say or do. Keep our eyes peeled. What more can we do, when any move we make's likely to get back to Marty? Warn him we know what we know? The only advantage we've got for the moment is he doesn't know we've found out he's got this source of his.'

'All right, I suppose.' Another half-mutinous look. 'But we can't go on doing nothing. It can't be much longer before that stuff comes in at the airport. And I've got a bit of bad news about that in any case.'

'What now?'

'It's just that it turns out that Norchester is the main point of import in all Britain for mangoes from South America. The security chief there told me there's scarcely a week goes by without a load or two coming in.'

Ned thought for a moment.

'Well, yes, that's a setback, true enough. So we'll just have to hope my source gets to know far enough ahead when the Corrigans plan to go in. He should do.'

'All right, but it's trouble whichever way you look at it.'

'There we agree. Only I happen to think the trouble'll be worth it. One hundred per cent.'

The big man heaved himself to his feet. Looked away.

'Oh, and Ned, speaking of trouble, you won't forget my Frank's precious Cindy?'

'I'll have her up right away. Let you know what it turns out to be about as soon as I've got it out of her.'

He delayed having his interview with Policewoman Cindy Grundy until after he had paid a visit to the Collator to ask about sightings of Gismo Hawkins. It had become a daily practice with him now, one he felt obliged to make in person rather than waiting till the print-out landed on his desk. Not that he had ever learnt anything beyond that Gismo was reported as being seen by beat officers or cruising detectives sometimes two or three times in twenty-four hours. But no one had spotted him doing anything out of the ordinary. He had been seen visiting clubs, working in the yard outside his tumbledown repair shop, driving battered old cars from Point A to Point B. No more.

Cindy, when he summoned her to his office, hardly produced anything to tell her father-in-law. She stood at attention in front of his desk, bosom straining at her uniform blouse, hips stretching the regulation blue skirt, bold-featured face sullenly mutinous, wide full-lipped mouth set in a fixed line, and listened to what he had to say. But, be sharp with her as he might, she would hardly even admit she was frequently absent from her work.

'Now, listen to me. DI Smithers tells me you're away from your desk time and time again. What are you doing? I want an answer. Or it'll be the worse for you.'

'I have to visit the toilet sometimes, don't I?'

'DI Smithers says you're often away as long as an hour.'

'Not true, sir.'

'Well then, how long are you out of the bureau?'

'It may be almost half an hour sometimes, I suppose. I've got women's troubles, if you must know.'

By way of silent acknowledgment of Deborah Brooke and her views he let that go.

'Very well. Now, listen to me. If it comes to my ears once more, just once, that you've been absent from your desk for any length of time, you'll be up before a disciplinary board. And, if I have anything to do with it, you'll be out on your arse. Understood?'

'Sir.'

He used the internal phone to lie to George Grundy about how it had gone. And made the call as short as he could.

Two days later Shirley told him, not without an edge to her voice, that 'that Ms Brooke' was on the line.

He picked up his phone.

'Ms Brooke?' Voice laced with coldness. Secretaries have ears.

'Mr French, I've had to come up to Norchester. On business. There are one or two points I'd like to raise with you while I'm here, if I may. I'm tied up at present. But could you possibly see me this evening?'

'Yes. I suppose I could manage that. Would you like to meet me out of the office? Say at the Red Dragon Hotel? About six-thirty? You know where the Red Dragon is?'

'Opposite the cathedral, isn't it?'

'That's right. See you there then. But I shan't be able to spare you very long.'

Are you listening still, young Shirley?

He put down the phone, and wondered whether there really were any 'points' Deborah had to raise with him. There could be. She was certainly not going to stop digging on behalf of Heather Jonas just because they had been to bed together. And should be again before long.

But Palmy. Time was passing and no sign yet that he had got hold of Heather Jonas's statement. Those six or seven sheets in his own handwriting with, not only the amateurishly forged time and date at their head, but – as bad, now it had been brought back to mind – those brutal re-orderings he had made of what Heather had actually blurted out.

Could those half-dozen neatly written, initialled and signed sheets have been lost already in the files down in Nottingham? Was that why he'd heard nothing from Palmy? The best possible ending to his worries. But not very likely. So was it just that Palmy was hanging about trying to make up his mind to go and rout about among those ancient files? Hardly a risky undertaking. But if any sort of risk could be avoided by doing nothing Palmy would do just that.

And what if—

The thought came in like a knife thrust.

87

What if Palmy had hung about too long, and Ms Deborah Brooke had got to the statement before him? What if she had a 'point' indeed to raise with him?

# 10

However, nothing of any consequence was said at the Red Dragon Hotel. Deborah's 'points to raise' must have been no more than a little cautious covering-up. Well and good.

So, after a quick drink they set off for Drambleham Manor where he had taken her before. Pricey indeed, but safe from prying eyes. So pricey, even the Heap Big Chief would go there only on special occasions. No one else in the force was likely to put so much as a nose inside. But, once it was plain Deborah had come to Norchester with no more than the intention of spending the night with him, in a sweat-flush of relief that Heather Jonas's statement was still a secret he had felt a decent dinner was the least he could provide.

The only reference made to Heather, just as they settled in the car, was to announce abruptly that, still ill, she had been transferred from prison to hospital. Otherwise they sat in silence – expectant silence? – as the hedges and houses to either side came swirling out of the darkness in the headlights.

The flaring sign of the Golden Goose appeared on their right. Was Peter Kitson there at that moment supervising the evening's entertainment?

'Isn't that the place you nearly took me to till you remembered it belonged to some criminal?'

'Quite right.'

'Comical, really, to think how little we knew each other then.'

89

'We don't know too much about each other now, Ms Brooke.'

'Well . . . I see what you mean, but in fact I think I know some aspects of you pretty thoroughly, Assistant Chief French.'

'Such as?'

'Such as what a hard bugger you are.'

'Oh. Thank you.'

'And how much good your being hard actually does. Well, in your work anyhow. I mean, look at the way you wouldn't even go near that place just because you'd remembered a criminal owned it.'

But he had hardly heard those last words.

For some reason, for none, the mention of the time he had sharply braked on the point of entering the Golden Goose's muddy, ill-lit dump of a car park had sent into his mind a camera-flash of recollection. The couple he had briefly seen in his headlights getting out of their car there.

The girl, he knew beyond doubt now, had been Cindy Grundy. Not until that night, as it happened, ever seen out of her constable's uniform, or, until he had had her up in front of him, ever particularly noticed. And the man beside her in the car park had not been George Grundy's Frank, whom he knew slightly but well enough. He had been one Detective Constable Terry Tucker. According to gossip, champion romeo of the CID.

And simultaneously the thought had come to him: what was Detective Chief Superintendent Grundy's daughter-in-law doing with a notably amorous colleague at an eating place well outside Norchester itself? Answer plain. The same answer that accounted for her long absences from the Fingerprint Bureau. Presumably on that evening Frank Grundy had been safely out of the way somewhere. Hadn't the fellow, the only time he had had any talk with him, at a party once, gone on endlessly about singing with the choir at his church? Damn it, he'd said they practised every Tuesday. Been a bore about it. And hadn't it been a week ago yesterday, Tuesday, that Deborah had come up to see him for the second time? When he had nearly taken her to the Golden Goose.

So, while Frank Grundy was giving full voice to Bach or Handel or whoever, his slut of a wife and her bit on the side had been stuffing and swilling before going to bed together.

Much as he himself was intending to do with Deborah now.

But, while there was no serious objection to ACC French taking Ms Deborah Brooke to bed, there was a very serious objection to Cindy Grundy two-timing her husband. Frank Grundy was the only son of puritanical George Grundy. *We should come down a sight harder on every whore in the city.* If the least whisper of her activities got to George's ears she would find herself divorced before she had time to pull her knickers back on. Very likely, too, she would be given such a hard time in her job that in a few weeks she would quit. So here was someone who had, in words he had used to George Grundy only a couple of days before, got themselves into a really damaging situation. *And in the end they'll feed out whatever they can.*

Cindy as the leak? And young Shirley, however much nose out of joint, good as gold. Poor kid.

But, yes, of course, those stupid reminders George Grundy was always making to himself on odd scraps of paper. Making, and often leaving lying on his desk. His desk in an office Cindy was in the habit of going to with messages from her husband, whatever. An office, once Marty Corrigan had got her in his grip, she no doubt entered on any excuse she could think up.

He was tempted to turn the car round, go back, get hold of Cindy wherever she might be. Have her put in a cell with a couple of tough old prostitutes. Let them know she was a policewoman. In a couple of hours she'd be ready to admit to her every last piece of passed-on information. And he'd do his best to see she got the maximum term after. Don't give the buggers one inch. Then there'd be a fine example for anyone else in the force with ideas about feeding information to the slime.

But in a moment second thoughts prevailed. Now that he knew who was leaking to Marty Corrigan, and while Marty had no idea he did know, a perfect channel was in place to feed the Corrigans whatever disinformation he cared to produce. One of George's notes, left lying where Cindy could not but see it, and within an hour Marty would have heard whatever it suited them to have him believe. Till this business was over Cindy could live on. Love on.

What they called good detective work.

And, what's more, there was already one piece of information he'd very much like the Corrigans to learn. That there had actually been a watch set on their house in the South End but that now it had been withdrawn. For once, George Grundy had not made one of his little notes of his order about that. Too knocked about by the bollocking he'd had. Well, he could wipe out that debit by scrawling something about the order after all. And by doing what he could to make certain his hot-arsed little daughter-in-law saw it afterwards. Making him do nothing to rouse the girl's suspicions when he'd been told what she had been doing would be a nicely appropriate disciplinary lesson, too.

And, once the Corrigans thought the lumbering Norchester police were no longer even trying to keep them under surveillance, they might feel free to give away more of their ultimate intentions. Yes, good detective work.

Deborah, it turned out however, did have one 'point' to raise that evening. Even if it did not require much answering.

She waited till they were drinking their coffee. Just as well. Time enough for him to have cooled down after what he had realized about Cindy Grundy.

'Ned, I think there's something I must tell you about Heather before— Well, before anything.'

'Oh, yes? Let me remind you though, you've already pointed out, not without a bit of edge, that she's now ill enough to be transferred to hospital.'

'No. Come on, no edge at all. I just mentioned it. I never so much as hinted her trouble was caused by her years in prison.'

'Okay, you didn't. But if you had – or if you are now – I'd have certainly suggested that her getting worse might well be because her hopes of being freed and pardoned and the lot have been raised and have got nowhere. But how bad actually is she?'

'It's just something that needs more looking at, I think, than she could get in the prison infirmary. She's not at death's door.'

'Glad to hear it. So what is it you think you ought to tell me *before*?'

She smiled.

'Just that I've had a bit of luck. I don't suppose you remember that on the night you and Detective Sergeant Palmer bullied that so-called confession out of Heather she was seen by a doctor?'

'No doubt she was. Standard procedure after a confession to murder. Even in those distant days. We never want it said in court someone was roughed up.'

'All right. But what you don't know is that the doctor who saw Heather that night, though he's been long retired, is still alive. And with his memory unimpaired.'

'So . . .?'

'He told me that when he saw Heather she showed plain signs of having been put through the mill.'

'Indeed? And just what does that mean, Ms Brooke? *Put through the mill?*'

'Not given anything to eat or drink. Subjected to a long and harassing interrogation by two police officers, with no one there to tell her of her rights.'

'Only that? What, not beaten black-and-blue as well? You disappoint me.'

If, he thought, that doctor, whoever he was, had paid any attention at the time to the marks of Palmy's swung handcuffs on the backs of Heather's hands, he had plainly forgotten them now. The jibe was safe enough.

And he had to keep his end up.

'Oh, what Dr Hodges has got to say about Heather's condition will be enough, believe you me. If she was in the state he described to me, then it looks clearer than ever that in the course of a long night's interrogation Heather's confession was simply bullied out of her.'

Then, quite suddenly, he remembered the man Deborah had got on to.

'Ah,' he said, 'Dr Hodges was the regular doc at Nottinghamshire HQ. He must have examined Heather when she was taken there.'

'Yes, that's him.'

'Right. Well, he was no sympathizer with criminals, I can tell you. Oh, he'd do his duty, check them over. But he was never one to produce fancy objections when anybody had been caught bang to rights. And no doubt he treated Heather Jonas just as he treated any other suspect. You'll find, if it ever comes to an inquiry, he won't be so ready to give the sort of evidence you hope for.'

He leant back in his chair, satisfied.

And then he realized what it was exactly that Deborah had said: *in the course of a long night's interrogation.* Plainly, then, old Dr Hodges had remembered what time it was, more or less, that he had examined Heather. And it had been nothing like within a couple of hours of the time, *8.13 p.m.*, inscribed in his own handwriting at the head of Heather's confession. No doubt, too, if

94

specifically questioned, Heather would remember, roughly, what time it was that she had at last been brought into the interrogation room.

And there, in some basement at Nottingham, that statement was safely stored, all ready for Deborah to get hold of. Unless by any happy chance bloody Palmy Palmer had done what he'd been told to do.

Should he go to a pay-phone, try and get through to the bugger now, this minute? But it wouldn't be easy. Deborah might suspect something. Even follow and listen.

They had been in bed for not much more than an hour. Their spat over Heather and Dr Hodges's examination all those years ago seemingly having been no bar to *before*. Which was now *after*. He had put out the light and was lying there on the verge of satiated sleep.

The phone on the table beside him buzzed startlingly.

He picked it up in the dark.

'French.'

'Palmy here, Ned. Hope I didn't get you out of bed.'

Calling now? At this time of night? And to the flat? This was no bringing of good news.

95

# 11

He rolled quietly out of bed, stooped, pulled the phone jack from its socket, crept with the instrument into the sitting room, softly pulling the door closed behind him. Even then he took the precaution of not turning on a light, feeling for the other phone socket in the dark. Keeping his voice well down, he spoke again.

'Right. Now, have you got hold of— Of what we talked about?'

'Here, someone in bed with you, is there? Always were a randy sod.'

He would have liked to put Palmy in his place. In no uncertain way. But it was plain enough even from that one answer that this was no longer something he could do.

'Listen, did you manage it? Come on, don't mess me about.'

'All right, all right. I got it. What else d'you think I'd be ringing you about?'

'I never expected you to ring at all. It was my address I gave you, not my phone number.'

'Yeah. Had to find that out, didn't I? Ex-directory French, E.J.'

'So you employed your detective skills, such as they are. Why?'

'Thought we ought to have a little discuss, that's all.'

'I don't see there's any need for any discussion. I explained why it was vital to get hold of— To do what

96

I suggested. And, once you'd done it and sent that to me, I saw no need for us to have anything more to do with one another. In fact, there's every reason why we shouldn't.'

'Oh, yes. Every reason. Suit you fine, wouldn't it, for no one ever to know you'd had to go scurrying back to your old mate Palmy. Suit you fine just to get hold of that statement and put a match to it. No one ever find out what ACC French did when he was just pushy DC French.'

'Now, look here—'

'But what'd be in it for me if you'd made away with that statement, eh?'

'You'd be just as much protected as I'd be.'

'I'd be just as safe as if it'd been me that got rid of it? That what you mean? But you didn't trust me for that, did you, Mr High-and-mighty French? Well, suppose I don't trust you either. Suppose I think that statement's better off with me. Intact.'

In the darkness of the sitting room he put his mouth even closer to the phone.

'Look, just see it from my point of view. All right, I admit you've been the one who's had to take the risks. But I've got a lot more to lose than you if that— that thing ever gets into the wrong hands. So I have to be a hundred per cent certain it's been destroyed, yes? So, all right. Listen, by way of recognition of the way the business fell out – your share tougher than mine – I'm willing to offer you ... compensation.'

'That's more like it.'

'I thought it might be. Okay, no messing about. Name your figure.'

'Bit more to it than that, mate.'

'What d'you mean? Look here—'

He stifled what he might have said.

'I'll tell you what I mean. Just this. The boot's on the other foot now. I'm not going to put any match to that

97

statement. Not when, safely tucked away with me, there'll be nothing you can do to drop me in the shit if it comes to an inquiry.'

'Look, Palmy, I've no intention—'

'Oh, yes, you have. Or you damn well had. You told me so, straight out. You said you'd never move one inch to cover my back. Well, you'll have to now, won't you? You'll have to move just as many inches as I tell you. Unless you want me to hand over that statement to the investigating officer, whoever he may be. Hand it over like a good boy, and point out who altered that time, that date. Against my better judgment. That's what I'll say. Against my better judgment. Mate.'

He thought.

'Well, we'll leave it as it is for the time being then.'

'Right. But there's something you promised.'

'What's this?'

'Shall we say a couple of thousand quid. Used notes, of course. And as soon as you like. You can send them to me at HQ. I won't open the packet in front of everybody. You can rely on that.'

The ping of a receiver dropped on to its rest.

He sat on there in the dark, his hand still on the phone.

Could Deborah have heard any of all that? And, if she had, would she have cottoned on? She might even have got out of bed. Put her ear to the door. Opened it a crack.

What had he actually said? He certainly hadn't used the word *statement*. It had been too much in his mind to have made that mistake. But he must have used Palmy's name. Almost certainly. So, if she had heard that . . .?

Yes, she'd put two and two together all right then. She must know that the statement he had taken from Heather – or she might think Palmy had taken it – ought to be still in existence. It was a wonder she had not

98

managed to have it dug out for her already. So she was almost bound to be able to deduce from the secrecy of that call, from Palmy first announcing himself, loud and clear in that twanging, fuck-you voice of his, from the way he had come in here to take the call, from not putting on a light, from things he had said or half-said, what it was the two of them had done all those years ago. To deduce, or at least make a damn good guess.

And then...?

In the morning would she leave, suddenly all uptight? And, before much longer, would the call come to the Great White Chief of the Homebodies? And... finis.

A thought stirred in his mind. Go into the bedroom this minute, tell Deborah the truth of it all?

Say that, all right, in his young days as a detective he had made a serious mistake. He had improved that confession Heather Jonas had made. Altered the time of it. Clarified things she had said that had been by no means clear. The car journey down from Tottle Brook to The Park, when she had never learnt to drive. The shopping-bag the bomb had been put in that was only a guess on the part of Palmy Palmer. More, that he had allowed Heather to skim sightlessly over what they had made her say before she had put her signature to those words, *I have read the above statement and been told I can correct, alter or add anything I wish. This statement is true and I have made it of my own free will.*

In none of that had he been doing the right thing. But if he was forced to admit to those errors publicly, he could tell her, he would be almost certain to be suspended. The press howling for blood. Perhaps he would be obliged to resign, whether on cooked-up, face-saving medical grounds or simply because he could no longer fulfil his duties. And if he resigned, if he was suspended, there would be no one who could learn from Peter Kitson what exactly were the Corrigans' plans for grabbing that immense cargo of cocaine.

He could say all that. And go on.

If, in actual fact, what Heather Jonas had confessed to under undue pressure was a crime she had never committed, it would be a different matter. But the truth was he could not believe he had made a total error that night back in Nottingham all those years ago. Not possibly.

Damn it, Heather had said then, clearly as clearly, *Reardon Smart deserved to die. I killed him. Yes, me. It was me.* He had believed, from the moment she had shouted that out, she was the person who had put that bomb under Smart's car and killed him and three innocent children with him. Nor had he had any doubts about it in all the years afterwards.

He stood up abruptly from the chair he had squatted on beside the phone.

But hadn't he just recently had tiny niggles of doubt? Hadn't there been moments when he had not perhaps absolutely believed Heather had been the person who had planted that bomb? When he had at least considered it just possible she had not?

And now this. That shit Palmy Palmer blackmailing him. Because that – face it – was what Palmy was doing. And he had had to knuckle under. Not exactly the hard man Deborah Brooke credited him with being. The good detective.

Yet if the Corrigans were to be stopped, he absolutely must be there to stop them. In place. So, no. No appeal to Deborah. A risk not to be taken, however momentarily tempting. To chance that this fixated crusader – lying in his bed now – would see his point of view. A point of view overriding any obvious, simple, naive notions about justice and its importance. Not to be hazarded. Possibly.

No, stay silent. Tough it out. The only thing.

He turned back to the bedroom.

In the bed, apparently a sleep-sodden hump, Deborah

lay on her side facing away from him, duvet hunched round her. She was not exactly snoring, but breathing deeply and regularly.

Faking?

It could be.

On the other hand, it did not sound like it. But, even if she was asleep now, had she been woken enough when the phone rang to realize who it was who had called? And now, tired out, however much she might have been thinking about it all, had she actually dropped off again?

He stood looking down at the heaped duvet.

Wake her up? Jerk her into consciousness? If she wasn't already wide awake and faking. Demand from her how much she knew? Use physical force?

But what would be the good of that? She was already aware there ought to be a statement in the files in Nottingham. If she now knew that statement actually contained something which had made him bully Palmy into pulling it out of the files, she would have that much more ammunition for her fight.

For a few moments longer he stood beside the bed, looking down at the humped figure. A bomb, when the timer clicked round far enough, that could blow him right out of his career. And blow away at the same instant all hopes of putting the Corrigans out of business, of pushing back the slime a long, long way.

A triggered bomb. Irony there all right.

But another phone call, in the darkness while the alarm had yet to ring, came before the moment when he would have to assess in the cold light of day what Deborah's feelings now were, whether she did have that extra ammunition.

'French.'

'Listen, I can't be long.'

Peter Kitson. Urgent and scared.

'Listening.'

101

'Can we have a meet straight away? The multi-storey, if it's open. Or outside. Outside it.'

'What's it you've got? Give me some hint, for Christ's sake.'

But before he had finished the sentence the phone had been clunked down.

God, if Marty or Barty perhaps at the far end had overheard that. If, for some reason, they were out at the Golden Goose where Peter was. Or if Peter was at the big South End house. They would have caught on without fail. *Can we have a meet?* Just those five whispered, hurried words would have been enough to say to either of them that Peter was grassing. And then . . .

He snapped the light on and was into his clothes inside three minutes. Deborah was still groping for her glasses, sitting up in the bed – white body, full lifted breasts – blinking in incomprehension, as he ran into the next room. But the moment he slammed the flat door all thoughts of her left his mind.

In the early-morning darkness outside the multi-storey he was able to make out Peter's Astra, parked, its lights out, fifty yards further along the deserted, pre-dawn street. He pulled up well behind, brakes harsh in the cold.

But, hell with protocol and keeping the upper hand, with hardly a glance to check on any possible watcher he jumped out and ran up to the Astra.

'Right, what is it?'

'The good news first, Mr French. I've got Lucy located.'

'Lucy? This is a hell of a fuss for not much worth hearing. Do you know what time of the morning it is?'

'Yes, I damn well do. And what I really got to tell you is: I'm going to have to close down. Marty's smelling a rat. I swear it. He's heard something from that mouth of his with you. Must have done. Must. You know what he said to me? Well, not said exactly, but just sort of mentioned. That he's paying someone at the Golden Goose, where I've got a little flat now, paying one of the staff to keep an eye on me. On me. When I never gave him no reason ever to think I wasn't hundred per cent on his team.'

'No, Peter, of course you never have. Soul of loyalty, bar our little arrangement.'

'Well, yes, Mr French. But I mean I couldn't help that in the first place, could I? Look, you know how it has to be now, don't you? I can't go on with it. I can't. Not one day more.'

'Don't be more of an idiot than you can help, Peter. I've told you. No one, but no one our side of the fence even knows your name. No one, bar me.'

'Well, yes, Mr French, if you say so. But then again, if that mouth Marty's got with you's been telling him you're on to things you shouldn't know, he's been thinking, hasn't he? And sooner or later he's going to start thinking definite about yours truly ...'

'Well, he won't. Why should he? He never has up to now. Not all the time down in London. Not up here. So just bloody forget about all that, and do what you're meant to do. Now, where's he put Lucy? At least that's something to have got hold of, getting up at this hour. Lucy's not at the South End house, I imagine.'

'They'll not have him seen within a mile of that, Mr French. You're right there. No, they've put him in a flat, down in what's called Pratts Town.'

'Address?'

'Mr French, you're not sending your boys there to pick Lucy up? Farty's there with him. Seeing he stays out of the limelight. If Farty got it into his head you knew where to look ...'

'I've not the least intention of having Lucy picked up. I just want to know where he is.'

'But you going to have the place staked out? I can't

take the risk, Mr French. Not now. Not with Marty looking at me the way he's been doing just lately.'

'Give me that address, Peter. Or I'll make damn sure Lucy and Farty know we're on to them.'

'Jesus, why do I let myself get into these situations?'

'Because you've been a bad boy in the past, my son, and now you've got to pay for it. So, that address.'

'Silver Street, Mr French. It's Number 18. Up above a launderette, I think.'

'You've not been there then? You've not see Lucy with your own eyes, damn you?'

'No, Mr French. No, I ain't. Tell you the truth, I'd rather not be around with animals like Lucy Luzzatto. Always fiddling with a shooter, and liking it. Just as if it was his willy, know what I mean?'

'Yes, I do know. And if you don't care for that sort of thing, you should have started thinking long ago about the sort of people you work for.'

'All right, all right. But if I did quit . . . Well, you'd be in trouble then for one thing, wouldn't you? Not knowing a blind bit about what's going on.'

'Now, now. Just watch your manners, my lad. I dare say I'd find some other nice gentleman to talk to if I had to. When we come across your body in some derelict house, maggots crawling out of your ears.'

'For God's sake, Mr French, don't say things like that. Not even in fun.'

'Who said it was in fun?'


He got back to his flat with, he thought, time enough to shave, put on a clean shirt, eat breakfast and, most important of all, sum up Deborah, before getting to the office. But Deborah had gone already.

Not even a note left.

He stood there, thinking.

Was this the uptight attitude he had been ready to find in her? Expressed by the total negative? If she had hardly been disturbed by Palmy's late-night call, had heard nothing, knew nothing, would she have left without any parting word? She might have done. She might well have thought whatever had sent him off just before dawn in such an almighty tear would keep him away till past the time for her train. The same 6.30 she had caught the first time they had slept together. And she might not have seen any need for a note then. She might, as soon as she got the chance, simply ring him. Suggest a time to meet again.

He got into the office eventually, shaved and breakfasted. But with less than ten minutes in hand.

As soon as he had dealt with the routine on his desk he rang through to George Grundy and asked him to step in. There was an awkward word to have with him. Best to do it as soon as he had put him in the picture about the flat where Lucy Luzzatto was waiting till his Luger was put into requisition.

'George, sit down. Couple of things to tell you. One, Lucy Luzzatto is in a flat down in Silver Street. Number 18, above a launderette. You might try getting a WDC in there, assistant manageress or something.'

'Will do.'

Hand to pocket. The inevitable envelope. The pencil stub.

'And now, George, something that's going to be a shock to you.'

'Yes?'

As much as to say, *I defy you to shock me, you poncy Southerner.*

'Look, I've found out who Marty Corrigan's got his claws into inside here. It's your daughter-in-law, Cindy.'

'What the hell—'

'By chance I happened to get a glimpse of her last Tuesday evening just as she was going into that restaurant the Corrigans have taken over, the Golden Goose at Markham. But it only came to me last night

105

who she was. She was out of uniform then. But the point is she was with DC Tucker. And Tuesdays are your Frank's choir night, George. Yes?'

A long moment of silence. A slow or slowish brain revolving.

'Tucker, that bastard. I never liked having him in CID. Come to that, I never liked having a sex-mad character like him in the force at all. But now he's out on his arse. And that little bitch with him.'

'No, George.'

'Oh, no, I'm not going to stand for any of your damned free thinking over this. With respect. Sir. For one thing Tucker and that girl have committed a serious offence. But in any case what they're doing should be put an end to. The force has got far too many sex-mad officers as it is. That sort of thing may be condoned in the Met, but we want no London looseness up here. Have you had this out with them?'

'No, George. I have not. And for a good reason.'

'A good reason? What good reason could there possibly be? Adultery. Fornication. It all goes together with assisting criminals.'

'George, just listen to me calmly, yes? There's a very good reason for my not having let Cindy know what I know. A good reason, too, George, why you're not going to tell her anything either.'

'There can't—'

'Yes, there can be. If she gets to know we're on to her, then it'll be us that's assisting criminals. Think, George. And I haven't told you yet how it is your Cindy learns as much as she does. But – and you've got to face this – it's because she's made a habit of reading those notes to yourself you're always making.'

Hand groping towards pocket. Red face slowly losing its colour.

'Oh, my God. Yes. Yes, I have caught her a couple of times in my office when she'd no particular reason to be

106

there. More than a couple of times, come to think of it. And once, when she didn't hear me coming in, I found her looking at the papers on my desk. I— I thought she was just nosey-parkering. But— Well, yes, Ned, I see it now. And— Right, I'm to blame. I admit it.'

'Look, I won't treat you as a kid, George. Those scrawls of yours were a breach of security. A damn serious one. But the good thing is they give us a fine chance now to turn the tables on Marty Corrigan.'

He saw George was beginning to get there.

'Yes, George. Let your precious Cindy see a note you've apparently jotted down, and whatever disinformation we choose to send Marty goes straight to him. And, what's more, I think I know what it'd be opportune for him to learn at just this moment. That we've taken the surveillance off that house at the South End.'

'But—'

'And then, George, they'll feel free to go about their business. And we'll reinstate the obbo. With people a bit sharper at the job than the last lot who went out there.'

It was a long moment before George Grundy gave his assent.

'All right. Yes, I suppose it's all right. I'll play along with bloody Cindy. For now. But I tell you I don't like doing things like this. If I had my way, Tucker and that bitch'd be looking at Forms 163 this very minute. There's a limit to how far you should go to catch criminals, even sewer rats like the Corrigans. My view, anyhow.'

'But not a view with enough balls in it, George. Not nearly enough balls. Not when you're up against the real slime.'

When George Grundy left he sat for a long while simply looking at his private-line phone and wishing it to ring. Even though Deborah could hardly be back in Nottingham this soon.

But no call came from her all the rest of that day.

And at home in the evening he would not let himself ring her. But he hardly left his chair beside the table with the phone, and instead of walking round for a bite at the pub round the corner he did no more than peer into the fridge and came away with a tin of beans. Which he spooned up cold. He succeeded in sleeping eventually. But only because he had swilled down the mouth-clinging beans with the best part of a bottle of whisky.

Next day he was hard put to it to concentrate on his work. It was, as it happened, mostly routine, and he managed to get through it without mistake. A heavy-faced, penitent George Grundy came in once and said he had left the false reminder for Cindy to see and would arrange new surveillance on the Corrigans' house. He had had a stroke of luck over the launderette in Silver Street as well. There had been only a temporary manageress there, and, for a consideration, she had happily agreed to take a holiday. The undercover substitute was already installed.

But that did nothing to lift his anxiety about Deborah.

Had she realized who had phoned him in the small hours? What the call was about? Had she, following up, spent yesterday attempting to see Palmy? Or had she simply told her Law Centre colleagues what she knew? And had that then gone to the Home Office?

Would the Chief be hearing from Whitehall perhaps at this very moment?

But if Deborah had not heard Palmy giving his name when the phone had buzzed, had not listened at the bedroom door to that long, furious, whispered conversation, why hadn't she called? Had she suddenly gone cold on him? Certainly no sign of that before bloody Palmy Palmer had rung. Far from it. So why wasn't she in touch? Why?

108

# 12

In the end it was not until early the following Tuesday morning that he heard from Deborah. His phone rang at quarter to nine, only minutes after he had sat down at his desk.

'Ah, you're in. I thought it was safe to ring about now.'

He hardly knew how to reply.

'Ned, it is you?'

'Yes, yes. It's me.'

'Listen, Ned, I'm sorry I didn't ring before. But I wasn't sure when I would be able to get away.'

'Oh, yes?'

'Hey, what's up? You sound sort of distant. Is there anybody there with you? You're not waiting for that mystery caller of yours, are you, the car-phone one?'

'No, no. It's quite all right.'

If she was going on like this, in this cheerful way, she couldn't have been busy all this time reporting his conduct to the Home Office.

He was in the clear. He must be. Friends again. Friends still. And so nothing now to prevent Peter Kitson feeding him the last vital pieces of information.

'Listen, did you say you were coming up here?'

'Yes, yes. I'm leaving as soon as I've got through a bit of work. I should get in to Norchester just after five. But ... Well, I should warn you, I'll be the bearer of bad tidings.'

Could she ...? After all ...?

He straightened in his chair.

'What bad tidings?'

'Oh, nothing too awful. But there is something I think it's only fair you should know. And I want to tell you face to face.'

Relief seeping down from his tensed shoulder muscles.

'That all you want?'

'Well . . . No. I do want to say I won't have to catch a train back till first thing tomorrow.'

'Ah. All right. So why not just take a cab straight to my place? I'll be there before you.'

Reassured, he had little difficulty in the course of that morning in putting out of his mind what was implicit in Deborah not needing to catch a train, and on the other hand what was threatened by the mention of *bad tidings*. There was plenty for an Assistant Chief (Operations) to think about and put in hand, even in cathedral-dominated Norchester. But what nagged and nagged at him whenever immediate work slackened was the thought still of the Corrigans. There lay a true menace louring over the quiet city he had pledged himself, at the moment he had first walked into his office, to keep cleansed of all the bigger crimes. Louring over Norchester and far beyond.

When was that disguised load of mangoes, one among the many coming in at the airport, actually going to arrive? Marty's visit there nosing about, duly clocked, had pinpointed well enough the place. But when exactly were the Corrigans and gun-loving Lucy the Luger going to raid whichever refrigerated shed that load was stored in?

And, when they came to ambush the Corrigans, how would it go? With all the unexpected eventualities awaiting? What if whatever major outfit in Europe owned the mangoes decided to mount a guard as soon as they arrived? With all the heavy fire-power they would have

110

at their command? A three-cornered gunfight? It hardly bore thinking about. Airport staff or members of the public wandering into lines of fire. Chaos of all sorts.

Then, even if there was no third-party interference, there were the everyday, still incalculable accidents that might occur. Key personnel in the Armed Response team suddenly falling sick. Guns jamming. Marksmen, always considered cool, mysteriously developing nerves. And, on the Corrigans' side, anything could happen, too. Farty going ape. As he well might, a totally wild element, unskilled with a weapon, seldom in control of himself and enjoying inflicting injury with whatever came to hand. Witness old Daddy Duffell's mangled body.

Unavenged Daddy Duffell. Unavenged because of his own decision to let the Corrigans have all this much rope.

A fierce desire came over him to go up to the airport that minute, and see for himself the exact layout of the refrigerated sheds. In no way an action down to the ACC (Operations). But all his old skills and practice clamoured to take it.

If he had firmly in his mind all the approaches to the sheds, knew exactly what security they had there ... then he could properly work out the most effective counter strategies. An ounce of preparation worth a pound of something-or-other. Tired cliché though that was, he found it to be true on dozens of operations down in London. Successful operations. Operations that had resulted in hard men being put behind bars where they could do no harm except to their fellow criminals. Or where they had ended up, once or twice, dead on the pavement. He had proved that time and again.

All right, George Grundy had seen the airport head of security. But George was George. There might be things that had escaped his attention. Questions he had failed to ask. Damn it, there would be questions he had not asked. And no point in hauling him over the

111

coals about what he might have failed to learn. He'd resent any implication that a chief detective superintendent from a northern force did not know his job as well as a jumped-up newcomer from the Met. Co-operation would be minimal after that. Dangerously so. When it came to that day up at the airport whenever it might be, something that ought not to go wrong easily could. Go badly wrong.

He half-rose in his chair. Slumped back into it.

But just before he was due to make his way to the senior officers' dining room for lunch, there did come one piece of good news on the Corrigan front. Detective Chief Superintendent Grundy at the door.

'My girl at the Silver Street launderette's turned up trumps. Thought you'd like to know, sir.'

Your girl. And who told you to get someone into the place?

'Oh, yes?'

'WDC Williams – good little copper there – radioed the car I'd got stationed nearby to say Marty Corrigan had come to the flat and had then left with Farty. Right?'

'Right, George.'

'So my boys followed Marty's vehicle. Nice and discreetly, needless to say. So, soon as I saw what route they were taking, I got a second car out there. Took over just as Marty crossed the city boundary. And where do you think that precious pair went then?'

'You tell me, George.'

'Out to Parbrook Forest, in the vicinity of Obelisk Hill. You know it?'

A little caution here. Had Grundy had a whisper it was to the Obelisk Hill crossroads that he'd once taken one of the force's old Fords? Was he hoping to discover who was his snout with the Corrigans? Office politics?

'I know where Obelisk Hill is, more or less. But I don't think I've ever actually seen it.'

'Well, all round there it's heathland. Plenty of cover from scrubby sort of trees and bushes. And the road's pretty winding. So my men in the car were able to stay nicely close. But then Marty took the turning that goes up to the obelisk and nowhere else. My boys had to stick to the main road, but they still turned up with something good.'

'I'm sure they did, George.'

'Yes, you see as soon as they were safe from observation from up by the obelisk they came to a halt. And, once they'd switched off the engine, what do you think they heard?'

Gun shots. Marty taking erratic Farty out to a really isolated spot to try and teach him to shoot straight. Or, probably more important, to get him familiar enough with a weapon not to cause unnecessary trouble by loosing off when he didn't have to.

'No, George, what did they hear?'

'Gun shots. Gun shots. Marty trying Farty out somewhere well away from human habitation.'

'I believe you're right, George. And you know what this means? Marty must have been given some sort of a date. It won't be long now. It can't be.'

'My thinking exactly.'

Deborah arrived at the flat – she had found a bus that took her from the station – only a few minutes after he had got there himself clutching a bottle of good white wine still somewhat chilled from the shop cabinet and the makings of a generous cold supper.

As soon as she had taken off her coat, she turned to him. A fencer with épée at the salute. And mouth-wateringly desirable.

'Ned, before either of us says anything else, I must tell you what I've now been able to do for poor Heather.'

On guard.

'Or not so poor Heather, depending how you see her. She still having an easy time in hospital? Or is she back in prison where she belongs?'

If it was duelling time, then go to it.

113

'No, she's not back in the prison. The prison where you put her, you and that Detective Sergeant Palmer who daren't even show me his face.'

Attack.

'Well, I rather think it was one of Her Majesty's judges who put Heather in gaol. When, let me remind you once again, she had pleaded Guilty to the murders she had been charged with.'

Parry.

'Yes, and why did she plead Guilty? Because of the treatment she received before signing her so-called confession. A statement which, as Heather's solicitor, I have every right to examine. And which I have so far failed to get sight of.'

Return thrust.

'Is that so? Well, I'm sure Nottinghamshire Constabulary is making every effort to find that ancient document for you. But, you must know, after fifteen years or so things are apt to get buried pretty deep.'

Blade deflected. Unscathed.

'And who sees they stay buried?'

Lightning thrust.

'Well, not an Assistant Chief with the City of Norchester Police, I can tell you that.'

Simply parried.

'And you expect me to believe there's no such thing as an old-boys network in the police? You were an officer of the Nottinghamshire force once. Don't tell me you haven't got friends there still.'

'Well, as a matter of fact, I haven't. No close friends. A lot can happen in thirteen or fourteen years, and it's that long since I left Nottingham.'

Hiss of blade against blade.

'But your Detective Sergeant Palmer's still there, isn't he? Detective Sergeant Palmer who conducted that abysmal interview with you.'

A dangerous play.

114

'Palmy? No friend of mine, I assure you.'

'But you've been in touch with him? Since you first heard from me? Was that what you were doing in Nottingham when you came to see me?'

Hot pursuit.

'You know very well what I was doing in Nottingham. And you were pleased enough, I think.'

Lunge.

'I'll thank you, Ned French, to keep personal matters out of this.'

Parry. But a hasty one.

'All right. So what is this you say you've done for *poor Heather*?'

Recover and attack.

'Right. It's that I've had another talk with Dr Hodges. Ancient old Dr Hodges. Whose memory of past events, however, is becoming remarkably clear.'

Blade darting, in threat.

'Oh, yes? And what has he remembered? Or what have you induced him to remember?'

Riposte.

'No question of inducing. I leave that sort of thing to police officers.'

A touch?

'Well, what then? Out with it, for God's sake. I want a drink before my supper.'

Yes, a touch.

'Just this. Dr Hodges is ready to go before any inquiry, or to give evidence in the Court of Appeal come to that, to say Heather Jonas was definitely the victim of physical maltreatment when he examined her that night, let alone that she showed every sign of suffering from undue stress. He'll talk about bruises on her hands. About signs of sleep deprivation. About the evident fact that she had gone for long past the statutory time without any refreshment.'

A hit. A clear hit. Disengage?

'Okay, you've told me what you wanted to tell me. So let's forget about it now. Let's have some supper. Do you want me to open the wine— Oh, damn and blast. It's been out of the fridge all this time.'

'Never mind. I'll have a whisky, if you've got it. We can eat when the wine's chilled again.'

It was much later when at last they ate, which they did sitting up in bed, the wine as cold almost as snow. But before Ned had fetched the bottle from the fridge they had talked again.

'Let me ask you something,' he had said, raising himself on one elbow. 'About— About Heather.'

'Yes?'

'I've been thinking. Trying actually to see things from the Deborah Brooke point of view.'

'And?'

'Well, what would be the situation if – I'm only saying if, mind – if it turns out that Heather did not actually plant that bomb?'

Short silence.

'Go on.'

'Well, supposing she really was innocent all those years ago, and you eventually got hold of some evidence to prove it?'

'As I— Well, never mind. What exactly do you want to know?'

'Well, what do you see as happening? In fact?'

'It's obvious, isn't it? The appropriate papers would go to the Home Office. The Home Secretary, or his advisers, would agree the case should go to the Court of Appeal. And it would. Heather would almost certainly be released on licence. And, after no doubt a wholly unjustifiable series of delays, the Court would find the case against Heather manifestly unsatisfactory. Judges' jargon.'

'Yes, I know all that. But Heather's not the only one involved, you know.'

116

'Well, yes, there's that man who actually did murder Reardon Smart and kill those children. But, I mean, he's dead. There's nothing anybody can do about him.'

'Safe from the vengeance of Ms Brooke?'

'No. No, not vengeance. All I want is to see justice done. And I mean to see it is, you know.'

'At any price?'

'Yes, of course, at any price. It's no justice if it's not worth sacrificing whatever has to be sacrificed for it. All the hypocrisies and the fudgings and the polite lies and face-savings have got to go. Otherwise we may as well give up. Let the jungle take over.'

'All right. I'll let that pass. But, listen, have you thought, really thought, what might have to be sacrificed? In actual fact. Not your nice vague *hypocrisies and face-savings*, but in actual concrete fact?'

'I don't quite see what you mean.'

'No? I said just now that Heather's not the only one involved. All right, you loosed off about that fellow who confessed to his gay friend—'

'Hey, that's not fair. You don't know they are gay, and in any case what does it matter if they are?'

'All right, high horse. I take back *gay*. But there are a lot more people who'll be affected than that lot if you get your justice for Heather Jonas.'

'Such as?'

'Oh, come on. Such as every police officer who had anything to do with Heather's prosecution.'

'Like Detective Constable French and Detective Sergeant Palmer.'

'Oh, yes. Like the two of us. We'd come in for most of the stick, I've no doubt. Though there are plenty of others who might find themselves in trouble. Officers who were far senior to me or Palmy Palmer in Nottingham fifteen years ago.'

'Most of them dead, actually. I got a full list of names, you know. Obvious first step in a business like this. And all the rest are long retired and not very likely to find

117

themselves charged with perjury. Or anything else.'

'As Detective Sergeant Palmer and Detective Constable— No, Assistant Chief Constable French are not. And will be very likely to find themselves targets of a Police Complaints Authority investigation.'

Another silence. A much longer one.

'Well, yes. Yes, but you've known this all along, haven't you? I mean, of course you knew what might happen the moment you heard the Heather Jonas case was being looked into again. But you knew it too when— Well, when you asked me to go out to dinner with you that evening instead of catching the train back to Nottingham.'

'Or from when you agreed to come. No hesitation.'

'Yes. Yes, it was like that. I admit it. So where does that leave us?'

New silence.

He broke it himself. Resignedly.

'Well, Ms Brooke, since all we've been saying rests on nothing but supposition, I imagine we're left precisely where we've always been.'

And he returned then, a worm of an unsatisfied something twisting a little within, to where they had been earlier. With an abandon that had in it more than a touch of desperation.

# 13

The week went by. From Deborah he heard nothing. Down in Nottingham was she, this time, actually assembling her evidence to send to the Homebodies? Did she now believe that, with what old Dr Hodges had said, she had enough? Before she had left on her usual early train he had asked her nothing. He had preferred not to go back to stirring muddy waters.

But her silence now, could it mean she wanted, knowing what she did, to cut the knot tying them together? As tightly as it had suddenly come into existence? Again, that was something he did not want to risk seeking an answer to. Not that there were not times when his hand reached out for the phone.

Yet, as day by day whenever he encountered the Big White Chief he found him amiably smiling, he began to believe there could not have been any sharp inquiry from the Homebodies. Deborah, or her cronies at the Meadows Law Centre, apparently must be reasoning that more was needed before they could present a case. Whitehall, they must have argued, would reject any evidence that could be brushed away. Too many miscarriages of justice in the past few years for them to countenance poorly substantiated suggestions that here was one more.

Heather's statement, too, with that damning forged time and date, was now out of Deborah's reach. The day after that small-hours call from Palmy, suppressing his fury, he had begun drawing out sums from cash machines and over the bank counter to add up to two thousand more or less untraceable pounds. Little though he liked the idea of Palmy in possession of that incriminating statement, there seemed no way of getting out of the situation. Bar a burglary of his own. Briefly contemplated, and dismissed.

On Friday morning he let his hand pick up the phone at last. A visit at the weekend?

'Listen, love, I can't get away myself. Something that may happen up here, important. So how about you coming to me? Say, tonight?'

'Let me think. Oh, hell, why not? Mr Important Assistant Chief Constable.'

It seemed that by unspoken agreement Heather's name was not to be mentioned over the whole time of the visit. It swam there submerged, inevitably. But at each occasion it threatened to surface, somehow it was kept under. By each of them. After the clash discussing Heather had led to the last time they had been together, no choice now but silence.

Not that another subject loaded with unexplored dangers did not begin to thrust itself into view.

'God, Ned, it's extraordinary to think we've only known each other just over a month. I was working it out the other day. We first met on March the seventeenth. I looked it up in my work diary. *Public holiday, Irish Republic and Northern Ireland. Nottingham: interview Assistant Chief Constable French.* That was all I'd written. And to think what it turned out to mean.'

'Right. The day a certain pushful lady made her way into my office and started bullying me.'

'Me? Bullying you? That's a laugh.'

'Well, if you didn't succeed, you had a damn good try.'

'But I didn't know you then. Not the real you.'

'Oh, yes? And what do you know of the real me even now, Ms Brooke?'

120

'Oh, quite a lot. Quite a lot. An extraordinary amount really, in such a short time. And you? You know an extraordinary amount about your Ms Brooke, don't you?'

'Well, yes. Yes, suppose I do. It's odd. Damned odd. Just over a month since we met and I think you're probably the woman in the whole world I know most about. Except, I suppose, for my much mistreated ex.'

'Tell me about her.'

He hesitated.

'Why d'you want to know?'

'Oh, I just do. She was the woman you were actually married to, after all.'

'So what? This another example of pure female curiosity? In spades, with you? Or is it—'

He stopped himself going on.

And Deborah, equally, seemed aware into what potentially dangerous territory this oblique talk about marriage was leading.

'Okay,' she said, rather quickly, 'it's a fact that I'm congenitally curious. I admit it. It's one of my great assets, actually. In my work.'

Out of one dangerous area into another.

'Just as— What d'you call it? Impenetrability is one of my great assets.'

'I'll say.'

He seized then on the safest way out of the quagmires they had neared.

'But I do have another asset, you know. Not much use for it at work, but . . .'

'So what's that?'

'Guess.'

'All right. Not very difficult. Not when you manifest it so crudely.'

Sunday turned out to be a lovely April day. Blue sky. Sun almost summer hot. Soft breeze. Birds. Flowers. The

121

lot. Deborah wanted a country walk. They drove out into Parbrook Forest, the only countryside round about he knew at all. At the familiar crossroads under Obelisk Hill he came to a halt and suggested going along beside the little River Par as it went through the clough and then making their way on up to the top of the hill.

No harm in working off a bit of the fat. Stuck at an Assistant Chief Constable's desk all day, nothing like as fit as he liked to be.

'Jesus, Ned, do you have to take that bloody machine with you? Out here?'

'What? Oh, the mobile phone. Well, yes. Yes, I do have to have it, however ridiculous it looks. But— Well, the business I mentioned when I asked you to come up, it may come off at any moment and I have to know.'

'What's it all about then?'

'No, Miss Curiosity. Shan't tell you. Ever. I haven't completely abandoned all Official Secrets Act promises, just because I've fallen in love with you.'

'Ned! Hell with the Official Secrets Act, you've certainly forgotten your famous impenetrability. I never thought to hear you say what you just have. Not however long we were together. *Fallen in love.*'

He looked at her.

'Well, why shouldn't I say it? It happens to be the truth.'

'Oh, do say it. Say it over and over again. I can't hear it too often. But— Well, it's just that I never expected you to put it into words. Even to let yourself think it, really.'

'Yes. All right, I didn't exactly count on saying it, on making it clear to myself, whatever. But it is clear, and I have said it.'

'So there, Ms Brooke?'

'Okay. So there.'

They climbed all the way to the top after that without a word said.

Even, puffed a little, up beside the tall tapering grey obelisk neither of them ventured to speak of anything serious.

'What was this huge object erected in honour of anyway?'

'I don't know. Battle of Trafalgar? Think someone told me that once.'

She walked round to where an engraved plaque faced the wide stretch of the heathland and an indifferent world.

'Hey, no. You're wrong. *Erected by Public Subscription in Ever Continuing Gratitude to John Churchill, Duke of Marlborough, Prince of Mindelheim, Victor of Ramillies, Oudenarde and Malplaquet Anno Domini 1772.*'

'Sounds like a real winner, though I can't say I know much about him. Must have had some connection with these parts, there's an Oudenarde Street just behind the cathedral. But my education took place mostly in the school playground, fighting. And coming out on top. Usually.'

'That figures. But surely you know what Marlborough's wife's supposed to have said when he came back from one of his campaigns.'

'If I was ever taught it at school I've forgotten.'

'It's not exactly a classroom story.'

'What then?'

'Oh, she's meant to have said to her best friend – I think it was the Queen – something like *My dear, he pleasured me thrice in his topboots.*'

He looked up at the tall monument.

'So that's why they put this monster phallus up.'

'Playground scrapper going to match the Duke's record by any chance?'

He looked all round. Not a soul in sight.

'He'll give it a go, can't say fairer than that.'

*

123

So it was tired but happy that, the car put into its garage, Deborah clutching his arm, he approached the glass-paned double doors of the flats entrance. And in the gathering darkness a voice hissed out of a clump of yellow-splashed laurels.

'Psst. Mr French.'

Peter Kitson.

He took a step towards him.

'What the hell are you doing here?'

'Mr French, I had to come. I've been waiting God knows how long. I daren't use the phone at the Goose no more. I daren't even go out to the phone box along the road. I think someone's watching me.'

'Damn you, Peter. You could have found a phone somewhere else.'

'But I might've been followed, Mr French. And you know what anyone'd think seeing me using a call-phone anywhere.'

'Oh, shut up, you miserable little whiner.'

He turned to Deborah.

'Listen, could you go on up and wait for me?'

'Certainly. If you'd give me the key.'

'Oh, Christ. Yes. Yes, here.'

He stayed where he was till he had seen her start up the stairs inside. Then he crossed over to Peter Kitson, still half-hidden among the laurels, and pushed his way in beside him. The street lights were coming on, and he did not want to risk even a chance passer-by seeing the two of them together. A constable on the beat who might recognize him and gossip. Or someone knowing a friend of a friend of the Corrigans.

'Now, what the hell is it?'

'Look, Mr French, if I embarrassed you, me being here when you was with the lady. Different lady from what you brought to the Goose that time. I'm sorry. But this is urgent. Vital.'

'Never mind the lady. If you've got something for me, let's be having it.'

124

'Yes, Mr French. Well, what it is: I overheard something. Marty and Barty talking, when they didn't know no one was there.'

'Okay. So . . .?'

'Well, they were saying, first off, how you lot knew the— The business what I mentioned that night at the Goose—'

'The raid, Peter, you told me Marty was planning the raid. For God's sake, we both know what we're talking about.'

'Yes, Mr French. But, you see, the thing is it's not going to happen where you think. That's what Marty and Barty were saying. Well, giggling about really.'

'Not at the airport? You're sure?'

'Yes, yes. You see, Marty was saying how he'd fooled your lot, going up to the airport and poncing about so he was bound to be clocked. And he knew you had a team watching the house, too, and they'd have been bound to see him go.'

'All right, yes. So Marty thinks he's made a monkey of us. Then where's he really counting on grabbing the stuff?'

'You'll never guess, Mr French.'

'I'm not in the business of guessing. I'm in the business of you telling me.'

'Yes. But it's at that crossroads. Where we met. Time I told you Marty had got a mouth in your place.'

'The crossroads down under Obelisk Hill?'

'That's it, Mr French. Right there. Funny, ain't it?'

Funny enough. His mind went back to the tall grey obelisk and what had happened beside it that afternoon.

'All right, Peter. You've done okay. I won't forget when the crunch comes. But just exactly when's the crunch going to be? If Marty's fixed on the place, doesn't he know the time?'

'He don't, Mr French, not the actual day. I heard him say that, too. *Soon as the final word comes through.* That's what he said. The final word.'

'Well then, just as soon as that does come through

125

you get on the blower to me. Never mind anyone hearing you or following you, so long as you keep what you say a bit wrapped up. But I want to know just as soon as Marty does. Not even half an hour later. Right?'

'But— But— Mr French, it's difficult. I—'

'Listen, Peter. Marty's biting off more than he can chew, yes?'

'He is, Mr French. He bloody well is.'

'Then if you don't want to find yourself caught up in it with him, you'd better see that I know everything I need to know. And as soon as ever you get the least whisper. Got that?'

'Yes, Mr French. Yes.'

At a quarter to six on the Monday morning, with only the palest early light showing through the gap in the bedroom curtains, as Deborah was beginning to get into her clothes to catch the first train south, they had something like a quarrel.

'You know I'm going on with it, Ned.'

'On with what?'

But he did know.

'With getting Heather freed. And I'll do it, you know. I'm certain once I get hold of that statement in its original I'll find something.'

'Are you indeed?'

'Yes, I bloody well am. Why else are so many obstacles being put in my way about seeing it? I've a right to, damn it. I'm preparing a case, eventually for the Court of Appeal, and I've a right as Heather's solicitor to examine something that may well be evidence.'

'Okay, then. Get hold of it. Make what you can of it. I don't think you'll have much luck, but I've forgotten what's there it was all so long ago. Anyhow, sodding good luck to you.'

'Oh, don't be so het up. You're only hiding what

you're afraid of. What I'm afraid of, too. If you must know.'

'Well, thank you for that.'

'Ned. Do we have to go on like this?'

'No, we don't. All you've got to do is shut up.'

'Okay, I'll stop. I'll stop saying anything about it at all. For now. But I won't stop doing anything about it. I can't. It's everything I believe in. Justice. Justice, Ned. And if it means— Well, if in the end it means you get hurt, well, that's how it'll have to be.'

'Fair enough. Fair enough, Ms Brooke.'

'Damn it, these tights aren't fit to wear.'

'Serves you right for lying about on the ground in them.'

'Sod you.'

At his desk later he was too caught up to have time to ask himself whether that spat of a quarrel had been a watershed or no more than a twist of an eddy in a steadily flowing river. Because if Marty Corrigan intended to make his bid for that millions-worth load not from one of the refrigerated stores at the airport but as it crossed bleak, deserted Parbrook Forest, then all plans had to be re-thought.

It would be a very different business having the Armed Response team lying out among the scrubby trees of the so-called forest rather than hidden at the vantage points already chosen among the airport transit sheds. Marty's descent on his booty would be a very different matter too. There would be no attempt to hold airport security guards to ransom. No gunning them down if they resisted. No blowing open the doors of whatever shed the mangoes were stored in. No bringing sufficient transport up to the airport without attracting notice.

Out at the Obelisk Hill crossroads, what would have to happen? He began to consider the possibilities.

127

About midday he called George Grundy in.

'I'm afraid bloody Marty Corrigan's played us for suckers, George. That sighting at the airport, it was no more than a piece of sodding disinformation. Heard it from my fellow inside their outfit last night. It seems Marty's aimed all along to ambush whatever transport the mangoes go south in out near Obelisk Hill. I suppose when your boys trailed him there he must have been doing rather more than teach Farty to use a gun. He must have been having a good look at the lie of the land. I wouldn't be altogether surprised, in fact, if that whole shooting business was no more than a blind.'

George Grundy's beard-shadowed face took on a look of sullen fury.

'I don't see that at all. I tell you, the lads in the car I had following Marty never saw him looking around down at the crossroads. He took the turning up to the hill quick as you like, and they began hearing those shots soon as he got to the top.'

'George, I'm not criticizing you or your lads. All I'm doing is telling you what I was lucky enough to learn from my snout. He overheard Marty and Barty talking about it. A first-class piece of luck for us.'

'And what if Marty was playing one of his clever tricks on you and your snout, eh? What if he meant the fellow to hear what he did? What if the boot's on the other foot with your famous disinformation?'

'No, George. If Barty knew for certain my man was leaking to me, there'd be no question of using him to play silly buggers like that. It'd be straight away *Farty, he's grassing on us*, and then woe betide him.'

'I don't see why Marty wouldn't play the same sort of dirty trick on us you thought you were playing on him. All that when you made me write on the back of an envelope that we'd called off the watch on the house at the South End. When I had to leave it to be seen by that bitch my Frank's married to. Same idea, same difference.'

128

'I dare say it is, in essence, George. But it so happens I am capable of playing things cool while Barty Corrigan, believe you me, is absolutely incapable of anything like it. All right, he'll let Marty try one of his clever tricks when it's just a question of him going up to the airport and prancing about till he's noticed. But, if he thought someone was grassing on him, I promise you nothing Marty could say or do would stop him setting Farty on the fellow. If he didn't beat him to a pulp himself first.'

'All right then. Since you know so much about a London thug like Barty Corrigan. But how about this? How about if your nasty little London snout's having you on? You can't trust a cheap twister of that sort. He'd shop you to Marty or Barty as soon as look at you. You know he would.'

For a moment the thought of that possibility hovered in his mind. It might be true. Peter Kitson was no angel.

But, no, what Peter was was a frightened man. Frightened that Marty and Barty were going to drag him down into something altogether too much for him. Too much for them.

'No, George. Take my word for it. My snout wouldn't dare play one of us off against the other. He hasn't got the bottle. You'll just have to accept my professional judgment for that.'

'You're the senior officer.'

It looked for an instant as if he was going to leave it at that. But he was incapable of suppressing the blunt Northerner in himself.

'But I'll say it once more. I'm damned if I think you're right. I'm damned if I think this whole scheme of yours is what good policing should be. Letting a load of London crooks play fast and loose with the law, all in the hope of bringing off some spectacular, career-boosting piece of— Of— Of bloody theatre.'

'All right, Grundy, you've had your say. You're not right. But I don't suppose anything I can tell you will change your mind. So give me your attention, please, while I explain what I see the situation's going to be out at Obelisk Hill.'

# 14

His private-line phone gave its sharp buzz. At once he felt the adrenalin pump.

Was this it? Peter Kitson at last? All right, there were a few people who had the number. But not very likely any of them would ring first thing in the morning. Once or twice in the past day or two the thought had come into his mind like a distant flash of lightning: bloody Peter's chickened out, gone over to Marty for keeps. But, no. No, here Peter was. Must be. With that one more thing he needed to know.

When.

'French.'

'Heather's dead.'

For a second or two he failed to take it in. That it was Deborah's voice he had heard, not Peter Kitson's. Even the actual meaning of what she had said.

'What— What did you say? It's Deborah, isn't it? It is Deborah?'

'Yes, yes. It's me. I'm sorry if I came rushing out with it. I— I've only just heard myself. They rang from the prison. The hospital had told them. Some sudden complication. Oh, Ned, Ned, I feel so bad. I— I don't know what to think. What I feel. What to do.'

'Take it easy, take it easy.'

The implications began to arrange themselves in his head.

'Listen, why don't you come up? I can't get away. That

business I told you about ... Well, that I told you was in the air.'

'What? Do you mean come now? Today?'

'Yes, yes. If you're feeling that badly about it, come up. And— And, well, we can at least talk.'

'Ned, I'd like to. I'd like nothing better. But ... Yes, look, I can't come now. I can't just walk out of the office. I've been giving too much time to Heather's case as it is. I've had more than a few black looks. But— But I will come for the weekend, if I may. I'd really like to talk. Yes.'

'Of course you may. See you tomorrow evening then? You'll be able to manage the same train as last week?'

'I think I might drive up, actually. Haven't got so much to do, now ... Now Heather's gone. Or— Or I don't think I will have.'

'See you when I see you then. I should be up at the flat by the time you get here. Unless this thing's begun. Thing I mentioned. In which case, you know the pub round the corner? The Wakefield Arms? I'll pick you up from there. Or leave a message.'

He was waiting in the flat – still no word from Peter Kitson, no sign of activity at the Corrigans' pretentious South End house – supper ready to go into the microwave, wine and a fresh bottle of whisky on the table, when Deborah's Volvo drew up outside.

But, letting her in, she seemed not even to hear his 'Drink, sweetheart? Whisky or wine?'

'Ned, I've been thinking all the way up in the car. About Heather. About what I should do now. And, listen. Listen, I'm sure, almost sure, that I shouldn't let her death make any difference. If justice had to be done for poor Heather while she was alive, it still has to be done for her now. I don't mean just to clear her name. If it was only that ... But I mean that justice is justice and it should be done, no matter what. Oh, and Ned. I know— I know it may affect you. Affect you badly, if I'm right in what I think may have happened, must have happened. But I don't think I ought to let that influence me. I mean, this is what I thought. That in a way, if it— if the outcome's going to hurt you, it will hurt me, too. Almost as much. But I ought to be ready to accept that. I must be. Ready to accept it whatever it may mean. To us. To what we— what we have together. That's what I think. That's what I'm sure of, almost sure of. What I worked out in the car.'

He let the whole flather of words pour out over him. He would have been hard put to it to halt them.

And he was unsure what his reaction to it all was. Even when he had sorted out from the wild whirl what essentially she had meant.

He began with that.

'Sweetheart, what you're saying is: you intend to go on poking away till you're satisfied you've found out the whole truth of what happened all those years ago in Nottingham when Heather made her confession to killing that man Reardon Smart and those kids. That's it, isn't it?'

It sobered her up.

She let herself sit. In the chair that happened to be nearest. She did nothing about taking off her coat, although the room was if anything overwarm.

'God,' she said, apparently seeing the bottles on the table for the first time. 'A drink. I could do with a drink.'

He poured her whisky without asking again if she would prefer wine. A good generous measure.

She took the glass before there was any question of adding to the spirit and swallowed a great gulp.

Then she looked up at him.

'Yes. Yes, that is what I meant. I think I ought to go on pursuing the case. I don't think Heather dying should make any difference.'

'I see. You know, I tried to stop myself thinking about

133

it until we'd talked. But really I knew you'd say that.'

'And— And you don't mind? It won't make any difference to us?'

'A difference? Another thing I prevented myself thinking about. But now I find I don't need to think. Of course it will make a difference.'

'But—'

'No, hear me out. I swore I would never tell you any of this. I swore I would simply hold my tongue whatever you found out, whatever your suspicions were. But I'm not going to. And there's a reason for that, a reason that's affected by Heather's death.'

He looked down at the whisky bottle on the table between them.

He could use a drink now himself. But, no, don't put it off.

'Look, first I've got to tell you the truth, the full truth, about that night in Nottingham.'

'Ned, don't. No. No, I don't know why, but I don't want to find it out this way. Not from you telling me, just because— Because of us.'

'But you're going to have to hear it from me. And now. Because there's a certain urgency. As I hope you'll come to see. But, first, just listen. Please.'

'Yes. Okay. Yes, I will.'

'Well then, this is what happened that night. As far as I can remember it. As far as I can remember it now, because, let me tell you, for years I genuinely hardly ever gave the business as much as a passing thought. At the time we handed Heather over to the top brass at Nottingham HQ, I absolutely believed we had found the person who had put that bomb under Reardon Smart's car and that we had induced her to confess to what she'd done. Do you believe that?'

'Of course. If you say it. If you say it the way you said it just now. No dodging. Straight out. Yes, I believe you.'

'All right then. So suddenly, after fifteen years or more,

I get to see in the paper one morning— No, actually I get to hear while I'm sitting in conference with my esteemed boss that there's a story in the papers. A story saying someone else, a man who had committed suicide, has confessed to being the one who planted that bomb. But even then I didn't believe we'd been wrong that night, Palmy Palmer and me. Detective Sergeant Palmer and Detective Constable, newly in the CID, Edward French. I thought that long-delayed confession must be a fake. A hoax, or some sort of malice. Whatever you like. But from that moment on I did begin to remember, very vividly, bits of it, some of what had actually taken place that night. I saw in my mind's eye things that had happened, re-heard words that had been said, in the course of those long hours of interviewing.'

He saw the beginnings of a question, a sharp question, in her eyes.

'No, let me just go on. Ask what you want after. What I remembered, then and at odd times since, was not totally reassuring. I remembered Palmy had hit the woman we were questioning. Not very seriously, no more than was acceptable, if not mentioned in public, in those days. No more than was pretty well customary, certainly with a known criminal if he was male. But what Palmy had done was to bring out his pair of regulation hand-cuffs, solidly heavy, and hit Heather's hands, which he had ordered her to place flat on the table in front of her. Painful of course, but not intolerably so. And at one moment he trod, hard and deliberately, on her foot. She was wearing wellingtons, a pretty wretched worn pair, and this was long before the days when detectives went about in trainers. So, again, it must have hurt her, though nothing like unbearably.'

He stopped then. Produced a wry sort of smile.

'You know, it was not until just a moment ago, almost at this very moment, that I remembered what my reaction was to that at the time. Thinking about it before,

135

when the hoo-hah you and those *Justice Watch* people were making brought it back to me, I just didn't remember whether I had condoned what Palmy was doing, or protested, or disagreed but stayed silent. Well, it was that, the third thing. There I was, a raw beginner as a detective, and there was Palmy already then an old hand. So if he did things like that, though I didn't feel altogether happy about it, not when he was doing it to a woman, I reckoned I had to keep my mouth shut.'

Now Deborah did break in.

'I understand that,' she said unexpectedly. 'Yes, it may contradict the image you've always given me, but I understand how you could feel that was wrong and yet acquiesce. I can see that.'

'Can you? So I'm not the only one not quite living up to their image, crusader-of-justice Brooke. But, all the same, I was a hard man by then. As a PC on the beat I'd had plenty of experience of the downside of humanity, and, well, I'd coined for myself a sort of motto. *Don't give the buggers one inch.* And what's more I still believe in that. Whatever you may feel.'

'All right. If you do, you do. But go on. More than what you've told me so far happened to Heather that night, didn't it? More than Detective Sergeant Palmer using physical force?'

'That night? There, to begin with, is something I've had to conceal from you whenever we've talked about Heather. And once or twice I came near slipping up. But I'll tell you now. It wasn't *that night* in the sense of it being some time after dark that we questioned Heather. We didn't begin, in fact, till quarter past three in the morning. But, at Palmy Palmer's urging before we submitted Heather's statement, I altered the time I'd written on the top. I changed it from *3.13 a.m.* to *8.13 p.m.* and adjusted the date accordingly. It happened to be easy to do without making it obvious something had been altered.'

He came to a halt. Another obstacle to be got over.

'And there's more. And, yes, this is something I'm bitterly ashamed of at this moment, though given the circumstances I'd do the same thing again. I'd have to. But just three weeks ago I went down to Nottingham – it was when I spent that night with you, lied about having to see someone about my alimony – and I got hold of Palmy Palmer and forced him into removing that statement from the ancient files.'

Now she was blankly unable to show any sympathy.

'But why? Why? Ned, that's criminal. A criminal offence. Stealing a police document. You know that. Why did you even think of doing it?'

'Oh, yes, it was a criminal act all right. Even more criminal in a way than I knew, as I've come to realize just in these past few hours.'

Again he stopped. The biggest hurdle of all to surmount now.

For just an instant he thought of saying nothing. Of fudging his way out of the admission he had begun to make.

But the full story had to be told. Had to be.

'You see, the thing is I'm convinced now that Heather Jonas never did plant that bomb. You've been right all along. She's innocent.'

He watched this sinking in. But went on before she could begin to say anything.

'So, yes, making away with a major piece of the evidence showing Heather's confession was extracted from her by a series of dubious acts was doubly criminal. Doubly.'

Deborah sat there, in her too heavy coat, the whisky glass still held in her hand, still as full as it had been after she had taken that one large gulp.

'You believe now Heather was not guilty?' she said at last. 'You believe that now, after all this time? And you really did think she was guilty before? You said so, but . . .'

'Yes, I said so. And it was the plain truth. Until I

heard from you that Heather was dead it had never entered my head— No, that's not true. Until I heard Heather was dead I had had only the faintest stirrings of unease about the case, and just in these last few weeks. Once or twice I had asked myself, half-asked myself, what the effect on her might have been of the way we— Mostly, to be strictly truthful, of the way Palmy questioned her. He had a damn crude way of more or less putting words into her mouth. And, if I didn't totally co-operate then, I certainly grabbed at anything incriminating Palmy made her say, got it down in that statement.'

'But now, for some reason, you're convinced you and that man Palmy forced a confession out of her to something she had not done?'

'Yes. Yes, that's right. Looking back now, I can see that even though Heather said clearly as clearly – I can quote you her exact words – *Reardon Smart deserved to die. And I killed him. Yes, me. It was me.* Even though she said that, she did not in fact carry that bomb down to The Park where Smart lived and put it under his car. I can see now what must have happened as we questioned her. Exhausted, hungry and thirsty and confused as she was, she suddenly saw it as her duty somehow to accept responsibility for an act she believed should have been done. She may have thought something like this – if you can call what was happening in her mind, thought at all – she may have said to herself, *If they had asked me to go with the bomb and put it under Reardon Smart's car, I would have done it. It's what I ought to have done. What I believe is right.* Something like that. She was a fanatic, you know. Whatever she was when you started to see her, she was an out-and-out fanatic back then. She believed her confession was a lie she had to tell. For the cause. Through thick and thin. Though I'll say this for her: at that moment, stuck away in a police-station cell as she had been, she hadn't heard at all

138

about the kids being killed. So she proudly claimed to be Reardon Smart's executioner.'

'But, Ned, why do you admit all this, see it all, now? Is it simply because Heather's dead?'

'No, no. How could it be that? No, I haven't all of a sudden come to see Heather as a sort of martyr. That'd be ridiculous. No, it's quite different. It's just, I suppose, that the shock of hearing about her death, when I'd had no idea she was anything but rather mysteriously ill, made me see that whole interrogation in a different light. Or in a light I'd seen it in for several weeks past but had refused to allow to come into my consciousness. Something like that.'

'Yes, at least I understand how that might happen. But, Ned, what about the theft of the statement? That's unforgivable. And— And where is it now? Can't it be— My God, you haven't destroyed it? You or your nasty friend Palmy?'

'No. No, Palmy's got it. And he'll hang on to it, too. He believes – and he's no friend of mine, far from it – he believes those sheets with my forgeries on them give him a hold over me. That I'll never attempt to shop him. Because, I see it now, he's known all along that Heather's confession was a cheat. He's known, and he hasn't cared a bugger.'

'But you. You do care, Ned. You've shown it in every word you've said just now. And all this can be put right. You'll do it, won't you?'

'No.'

He saw her jerk back as if that single blank syllable had been a hand landing slap across her face.

'No, listen. There's a reason why it has to be kept absolutely secret that Heather's confession was obtained the way it was. A good reason. A very good reason. I said I'd got something more to explain to you, and this is what. I cannot at this moment risk being suspended, or made to resign or put out of commission in any way.

I'm needed. Needed here. Vitally needed, as a matter of fact. At just this time. I told you there was something important in the air, didn't I? Why I took my mobile phone with me up Obelisk Hill. I believe I also told you you'd never learn from me what it was. Well, you're going to learn now. I'm going to make an appeal to you. An appeal to forget everything, everything I've just said about Heather Jonas.'

'But, no, Ned. No.'

'Yes. Listen, blast you, listen. At this very moment perhaps, somewhere in Norchester, a criminal gang – criminals, you understand, slime, people who think nothing of beating others to a jelly, of using guns, shooting to kill – a gang like that may be setting off to snatch from another criminal organization a consignment of cocaine that could make them millions. I mean that. Millions of pounds. Selling to the weak and the stupid. Wrecking countless lives.'

He was glaring at her.

'Do you have some idea how vicious people like that are? Or is every criminal in your eyes a sad case needing protection from the brutal police?'

'That's nonsense, and you know it. Just because I took up Heather's case – Heather whom you've admitted now was innocent of everything she was charged with – it doesn't mean I don't recognize there are criminals. Who should be put away, even. So don't try that on me.'

'All right, all right. But you say *who should be put away*, yet have you truly thought how they get put away? It's by us, the police. By, in this particular case, me. Because it so happens that we'll never get to know when that consignment of cocaine comes in, when it's due to be hijacked, unless the informant I have inside that gang, a man who won't trust anyone but me, gives me the word. You've seen him actually. The other night when he hissed at me in his silly melodramatic way from the laurels outside here.'

140

'Yes, I remember of course. I meant to ask you about him, but somehow knew I shouldn't.'

'Right. You shouldn't have done. People like him need secrecy, all they can get. But now I'm breaking that secrecy. To make you do what I'm asking. This fellow – and I won't give you his name, even now – this fellow will speak only to me. I've known him a long time, down in London, and to be frank I've got a hold on him. Because he's sung to me he's obliged to go on singing. But he's risking a hell of a lot to do it. His life, even. Quite likely his life. So if we in the police are to stand a chance of knowing when that mob is going to go for that huge load of drugs where we'll be able to catch them bang to rights, I've got to be around. Not just to hear from him, but to set in motion whatever's needed once I do hear. So that those evil men can be put behind bars for—'

He gave a grunt of a laugh.

'For as long as Heather Jonas was, or longer.'

She did not respond at once. But at last she lifted her head and looked straight at him.

'Yes, Ned, I see what your dilemma's been. All along. Since the time we first met, or before. And— And, much though it goes against the grain, against everything I believe in, well, I agree. I forgive you, Ned— Oh Christ, that sounds bloody pretentious. But I do forgive you, yes. For what you did to Heather all those years ago, for what you did to— To justice when you got that statement stolen. I see what you've had to do, and I agree to you doing it, to your having done it, whatever it is. I won't say a word to anyone about what you've told me. Ever.'

He didn't know how to express his gratitude. Even whether gratitude was what he ought to be expressing. Was it something else? Something deeper? But all words seemed ridiculously inadequate. How absurd to mutter *Oh, thank you* when she had fought down all she had believed in about Heather Jonas and her imprisonment.

All she had believed from even before they had met. Her life's beliefs.

For an instant he had contemplated simply taking her in his arms. But to reward her for that mind-reversing sacrifice with a good fuck seemed even more despicably cheap.

He took up the whisky bottle at least to pour a sort of libation on to the drink in her glass.

But she forestalled him.

Rising to her feet, shoving aside the coffee table in front of her, she took one stride towards him and extended wide her arms, still wearing the coat she had arrived in.

Then, murmuring from their hard-clasped embrace, came her voice.

'Ned. Ned, you did say, there going up that hill to where you trod in the great Marlborough's footsteps, you did say you loved me. Ned. Ned, I love you. Ned, we could ... Ned, it can be, can't it, more than just a quickie, an affair. Ned it can be something, you and me, as long as we ever are. Yes?'

'Yes,' he said.

# 15

His door was thrust open and George Grundy marched in.

'Something I think you might want to know, sir.'

*Sir?* What was this?

'Yes, George?'

'Report of a GBH victim I think may mean something to you.'

He knew at once who it was going to be. Peter Kitson. Everything Peter had said to him about his fears that Barty Corrigan somehow knew he was grassing came sharply into his head. Every single heartless slap-down joke he'd made to him about what might happen if he was right.

But why should it be Peter? Grievous bodily harm was inflicted on people quite often, even in staid Norchester. Victims of drunken brawls left lying unconscious. Wives sometimes beaten up and turned out into the streets. Young men who had come off worst in football gang skirmishes.

Yet why was George Grundy thinking this one more or less routine occurrence should be reported to his Assistant Chief Constable (Operations)?

'Well? Tell me.'

'Man of about forty found in the car park behind the Golden Goose restaurant out at Markham. Been very well done over. Luckily a cowman going to do his early milking just happened to hear a groan, went to look.

And the constable out at Markham while he was waiting for the ambulance caught a couple of muttered words. *Mister French.* That's what the PC said it sounded like.'

'I see. And, well, yes, George, you did right to let me know. Sounds very much like my snout with the Corrigans. Where is he now?'

'They brought him into St Winefride's. I've sent a DC to sit by the bedside. But they don't think he'll be saying anything more than those two words for a long while yet. If ever.'

'I'll go, though. It may not be my fellow after all.'

But, when he got to an intensive-care ward at St Winefride's, it was Peter Kitson he found, lying on the stiff white sheets of a white-painted hospital bed, the long tube from a drip dangling from above him, wires running to a slowly pulsing heart monitor near at hand. Peter Kitson no longer merely wan-faced but, where the lacerations and bruises left any untouched flesh, drained of the least hint of colour.

He turned to the nurse hovering at the bed's foot.

'What do they think? Can he pull through? Is it likely he'll be able to talk?'

'Certainly not for hours yet, sir. Serious but stable, that's the best we can say.'

'Right. Well, this officer will remain here in case there is anything he mutters, and we'll be sending an armed man shortly.'

The suddenly frightened look on her face.

'Now, I want to be informed, me personally, Assistant Chief Constable French, the minute there's the least sign of him coming round. Right?'

'Yes. Yes, sir, of course.'

Back to his Monday morning desk. And work to be done. If, he thought with seething anger, you can call work the shifting of papers, the reading, shrugging,

144

initialling and passing back down the line that goes by the name of administration.

Was this what I saw myself doing, long ago when I began to have a notion of where I could get to? Of how there was slime on the streets, and how a good detective could seriously bugger it. Keep it, if only for a while, under control. Was I all along slated to become this? A one-man admin factory.

Damn it, I ought to be out there. Catching villains. Tracking them down. Hauling them in. Even standing up in court and delivering evidence in a way no conniving lawyer can find a crack of fault in. So that the ones who prey on poor old simple John Public are put where they ought to be. Behind bars.

As the Corrigans should be. For what they've done to Peter. No innocent simpleton, but one of the weak certainly. For what Marty and Barty, most probably, had allowed Farty to do to Peter.

But would they now ever be put behind bars? That savage battering was a victory for them. No getting past that. Whether they had proof Peter's been grassing them, or whether it was only typical paranoid suspicion, the fact is there's now no fine string of communication running out to me from the inner workings of that power-mad, money-mad, evil lot.

How, now, can I find out when that cargo of cocaine hidden in all those carefully disguised mangoes is due up at the airport? How will I know, more vital this, when that load is going to be put into some container lorry and driven off, destination Europe, through deserted, made-for-it Parbrook Forest? Down under Obelisk Hill to be hijacked? How am I to get enough warning to put marksmen on the ground before that happens? So I can take the Corrigans in the act? Get them so tied down by incontrovertible evidence that they'll spend the rest of their lives, all but, in gaol?

Still something that could be done, of course. Double

the liaison with Security at the airport. Make sure every single time a cargo comes in with mangoes on the waybill it's reported back to us. Always provided the sheer amount of checking and cross-checking doesn't turn out to be more than they'll agree to. Check on the destination of each bloody outgoing load. Have trucks and container lorries followed. If there's the manpower to do it. Which there isn't. If the Big White Chief will authorize the expense. Which he won't. Unless he's told the full strength. When God knows what he'll do.

Perhaps stick-in-the-mud Grundy's right. Should we just content ourselves with identifying the right mango cargo, if we can? Seize it and congratulate ourselves on a good day's work done? That's the way Norchester's been policed up to now. And something to be said for it. But things became different the day a removals van arrived at that damn new-built, all-mod-cons and fartarsy gimmicks house out at the South End. The day the Corrigans arrived and cast a greedy eye all round.

Let the Corrigans go their own sweet way now? Laughing? Never.

But stopping them's not going to be easy with Peter out of account. Not by a long chalk. Even if eventually Peter comes out of it more or less intact. What will he be able to tell me days from now, weeks even, that'll be any use?

Four days later his bedside phone rang at 2 a.m., just past.

'French.'

'It's me, sir, DC Young at St Winefride's. I was told you wanted to know about Kitson, soon as he's fit to talk. They said any time, sir.'

'Stop blathering, Young. Is he talking? Has he said anything? What's he said?'

'He's asking for you, sir. Far as me and the nurses can make out. He's in and out of it, sir.'

'Ten minutes. Fifteen at most.'

He made it in nine.

Peter Kitson looked no better than when he had seen him last. Still lying flat in the white bed, looking as if he had been painted on to the white pillow, the stiff white undersheet. Still with the tube and the wires running down to him. Face still a mass of counter colours, if now deeper and darker in hue. The few patches untouched seemingly as drained of life as before.

But his eyes were open. Looking up at the blank ceiling above him.

Until this minute he had never really noticed how pale the blue of those eyes of his was. Doubly, trebly washed-out.

But perhaps that was the effect of the merciless battering Farty had inflicted.

'Hello, Peter. They tell me you're back with us again.'

'Mr French.'

Each of the three syllables separately dragged out. Immense fatigue lingering in each sound.

'I'm here, Peter. Here. Did you ask to see me?'

'Farty. He done ...'

'Yes, yes. We thought as much. Farty's work. And if it's any consolation we'll get him in the end. He'll pay some day, Peter. He'll pay.'

'Can – pay – now.'

'Now? Now? How? Tell me. Tell me, if you can. Take your time. I've got all night. All day, too, if you want.'

'Just – one – thing – tell. Marty – tricking ...'

The pale, pale blue eyes gently closed.

He darted the nurse by the foot of the bed a quick, urgent look. She did not seem worried.

And – flicker, flicker – the eyes opened again.

'I'm here, Peter. I'm still here. Tell me. Some trickery of Marty's?'

'Not mangoes.'

Had he heard what he thought he had heard?

147

'Not mangoes, Peter? Mangoes?'

'Marty . . . idea.'

A new silence. But this time the pale eyes stayed open. On the bruised features the effort to gather new strength plainly visible.

He waited, looking hard down into those pale eyes. Willing strength back into them.

'Marty – plan. Fill up that Daddy Du— Dad Whatsit. Cock-and-bull . . .'

'Marty gave Daddy Duffell some cock-and-bull story? To tell to us? To whoever pulled him in? To me? Is that it, Peter?'

'Yeh.'

For a while Peter seemed to be thinking he had done all he needed to. Eyes blank, unseeing. But after a little meaning came back into them. He even made a slight effort to raise his head.

'Didn't tell Farty. They never. But he found out. Daddy Whatsit grassing. Thought was. Done him. Done over. Dead. Said he was . . . Is . . .?'

'Yes, Peter, yes. We found Daddy's body. We guessed it was Farty's work. But he didn't do for you, did he, my son? Too tough for him you are.'

'Just – luck.'

Then for a minute, another minute, one more, far-from-tough, ever frightened, ever frightenable Peter Kitson lay there. Meditating perhaps on the luck that had preserved him from the fate meted out to Daddy Duffell. Or perhaps lost in vague, floating, ungraspable cottonwool thoughts.

At last he seemed to be coming back again.

'Peter, you said Marty planted a story on us through poor old Daddy Duffell. What story was it, Peter?'

'Story.'

A blank word.

Then a stir more of returning force.

'Mr French. I . . . Was going go back. To Barty, Marty. My mis—. . . My mistake.'

148

A silence now.

'Not quite with you, my son.'

'Like idiot. Thought Marty, Barty best bet. Not going to tell . . .'

'All right, my son. We all make mistakes. We all sometimes think the other lot'll do better by us.'

For a moment his own concentration slipped. The thought of Deborah intruded. Had he made the mistake of going over to her side? Or of dragging her across to his? He pushed it all down.

'Peter, all right, you thought for a bit you'd be safer staying with Barty and Marty, keeping their secrets. Well, yes, a mistake. You've found that out now, haven't you? But, listen, you said you could make Farty and the others pay for what he did to you. So do it, Peter. Make them pay. Now.'

And the snap of command did the trick.

'S'not— Not in mang— Beans. Green. Them.'

He saw it at once.

'Peter, you're telling me the cocaine's going to be hidden – this it? – in cases, crates, whatever, of green beans. Is that it, Peter? In green beans.'

'Yes.'

One word only. But said with an altogether new decisiveness. An affirmation of the simple truth of what had been said.

'Let me get it absolutely right, Peter. The stuff's coming in, just as you always said it was. But it's not going to be in crates of mangoes, but in crates of green beans. Jesus, I'd no idea beans were coming from South America now. But, never mind that, is the rest of it the same? Barty going to go for it on its way out, yes? At Obelisk Hill crossroads? That it, Peter?'

'Yes, Mr French.'

'And he'll be taking Lucy the Luger along?'

'Yes, Mr French. Yes.'

'And when, Peter? When's the stuff coming in? The

green beans? And when's it starting off on its way? What time, Peter?'

'No, Mr French.'

'No? No? What d'you mean, *no*? You're not holding back on me, Peter?'

'No, Mr French. No, no. Just don't know. If stuff's here yet. Marty don't know . . . think. But must be soon now. Mr Fre— Very, very soon.'

Eyelids slowly covering pallid blue eyes in utter weariness. End of conversation.

George Grundy had to be told. It was a few minutes after nine when he came in.

'My Peter Kitson's been talking, George.'

'That grass. I wouldn't give a button for anything he's said.'

'Oh, I don't know. I offered him revenge for what Farty Corrigan did to him, and he lapped it up.'

'No more than I'd expect from one of that sort. But how much can you believe, what he said?'

'I have to be the judge of that. But when someone's as physically weak as he was they don't have the guts to tell a good lie.'

'Well, that's your judgment. So what did he say?'

'Seems we've been the victim of one of Marty Corrigan's little jokes for a second time. First his airport walk-about, now Daddy Duffell. What seems to have happened, as far as I can read it from what Peter Kitson was able to say, is Marty loosed off about South American mangoes in front of Daddy as a deliberate ploy. Fed him plenty of whisky as part of it, pretended to feed it to himself and Barty as well. So Daddy left thinking the pair of them had got tight, said more than they meant to. And, of course, Marty arranged that breaking-and-entering episode up by the Chief's house, so we'd be bound to pull Daddy in. All-out effort.'

'Look, I can't believe this.'

150

'Well, I do now, George. I've been up all the rest of the night after Peter came to, working it out. It was a bloody elaborate scheme. Marty must have fixed it with that car maniac Gismo Hawkins. To put the notion into old Daddy's head that he could get himself out of a two-stretch, or whatever, by spilling to us. To you, actually. Cunning as you like. But it worked. Fooled us. Totally.'

'No, I'm sorry, I just don't believe it. Look, I knew old Daddy. A criminal, yes, but, damn it, a sort of friend. I knew him too well to let him fool me that way.'

'He did though, George. Believe you me. Or rather Marty fooled you, using old Daddy. Let it be a lesson never to trust a criminal, not even one like Daddy. Lesson to us both, though I should have known better.'

He got a dully belligerent glare for that.

'All right then, so what was Marty Corrigan attempting to plant on us? If he's so clever.'

'Simple, George. The mangoes. But mangoes are out. That's the guts of what I learnt from Peter Kitson. Mangoes are out.'

'What the heck does that mean? Whole thing's off now, is it? Good job, too, if you ask me. I never liked it.'

'No, George. The whole thing's on. In spades. We know now the stuff's going to come in, not as a load of mangoes but as a consignment of green beans.'

Visible disappointment on the ruddy, already beard-darkened face.

'Yes, green beans. And I've been on to your mate, head of security at the airport. Tells me that green-bean imports are a new thing, from Latin America. They get only a few cargoes up there, many fewer than mangoes. So it'll be easy enough for them to let us know when each one arrives. George, now we know what we're looking for, we know the place – Obelisk Hill still, Kitson says – and we know, near as damn it, the time. Very soon. So what I want from you, quick as you like, is a fully updated report on covering those crossroads. Men,

151

dispositions, weaponry, everything. We're going to get the Corrigans, George. If it means shooting every one of the buggers dead.'

A long moment of sullen rebelliousness before the answer came.

'Very good, sir.'

# 16

It was going well. Incredibly each of the obstacles that had seemed to tower up in front of him, looming, impassable, had been puffed away.

The sullen cloud, present in his mind from the moment long ago when young Shirley had called through to him that a Ms Deborah Brooke was on the line wanting to speak on a personal matter, had been dissipated. At a cost of more mental turmoil than he had experienced perhaps in all his life. But nonetheless it had now vanished. Certainly those few minutes face to face with Deborah that had ended with her promise of silence about Heather Jonas had meant more to him than all the rows leading up to his divorce, than all that had gone on between him and Myrtle in the days when he had first thought he was in love with her. But that fraught exchange – had it really not lasted very long, ten minutes, a quarter of an hour? – had finally ended the threat which, by her very uncompromisingness, Deborah had held over him.

The *Justice Watch* programme, which had once looked as if it might point the finger at him in a way that could not be laughed aside, had turned out to be so much journalistic hot air.

Daddy Duffell's death, which might have brought George Grundy to the point of open rebellion – or, worse, covert going behind his back to the Great White Chief – had fizzled away into muffled grumblings.

Palmy Palmer had been made to do what had been needed about that telltale statement, and then had been at least neutralized. If at a cost both financial and in injured pride. He presented no immediate danger. When the Corrigans had been arrested and charged, if the stand-off was still poised there, no doubt something would occur to him that would fix that sly bastard once and for all.

And now, when with the discovery of Peter Kitson more dead than alive in the car park at the Golden Goose all had seemed lost again, the situation had been abruptly reversed. Now he knew. Place, method. Only the final exact time had yet to be ascertained. As it very likely would be: when a message came from the airport that green beans were on the menu.

So, after everything, the Corrigans were almost under his hand.

He pushed himself up from his desk, gathered together the papers he might need, set off humming with suppressed cheerfulness for the routine end-of-week conference the Chief held with him and George Grundy.

He found the Chief in uniform, back from some official occasion. It seemed to give him a sense of extra importance. Braided cap and leather-bound stick on the desk in front of him. White moustache neat from brushing. Eyebrows echoing it.

'Well now, gentlemen, this business of the Corrigan gang. Those people have been up here long enough, you know. I hear comments. Complaints. There are rumours in the city about just what sort of individuals they are. I don't like it. Can't we do something positive about them?'

Without pausing to hear an answer he turned to George Grundy.

'Is there anything you've been able to get hold of, Mr Grundy?'

'No, sir.'

154

Very neutral, bitten-off answer.

'Mr French, this informant of yours, is he giving you anything? You're not holding something back from Mr Grundy, I hope.'

'The fellow's actually in hospital just now, sir.'

'In hospital? Is he ill? Or what is it?'

An unusually pernickety mood this afternoon.

'He was the victim of an attack, sir.'

'An attack? What sort of an attack? Why haven't I been told? What is all this about? I must be kept informed of such happenings.'

'I didn't think it was a matter worth drawing to your attention, sir. It's the sort of thing any snout may expect to encounter.'

'I dare say. I dare say. But there must be more to it than that. Do these Corrigan brothers suspect this fellow of yours of informing on them? Is that it? Are they responsible for this assault? Was the man seriously injured? Is there anything behind this I should know about?'

Of course there is. But too early still to give you a chance of aborting the whole operation. Fuddy-duddy.

'They're cousins, sir, actually, the Corrigans. Three cousins with the same name.'

'I don't want to know about their relationships, Mr French. I want to know how serious this assault on your informant was. You say he's in hospital?'

'He was attacked in a very vicious manner, yes, sir.'

'Then why has nothing been done about it? I dare say the fellow is no more than a wretched nark, but he is one of Her Majesty's subjects nevertheless. He is entitled to just as much from us as— As— As anybody else.'

'Yes, sir. But he has not actually made a complaint against any named individual. We may have a pretty good idea who was responsible. But, as you will appreciate, that's scarcely enough to warrant making arrests.'

'I dare say not. I dare say not. But is that the real

155

reason why you have hesitated to act? You're not waiting till these Corrigans launch into some major villainy, are you? I know that sort of thing's done in London. Letting criminals get away with comparatively minor offences in the expectation of taking them in the commission of some crime that will earn them stiff sentences. But I won't have it here. If these Corrigans were responsible for assaulting this person, then they should be dealt with.'

He shot glances from one of them to the other. Eyebrows drawn bristlingly together.

'Is that the situation, gentlemen? Are you, either of you, holding back deliberately? Mr French, are you importing these methods from the Met into Norchester?'

Time to speak out. Nothing else for it.

'Yes, sir, I have been.'

'Hah, I suspected as much. Well now, give me the full details. All the circumstances. I will not be tricked into running this force in complete ignorance of what is being done in my name.'

'Of course not, sir. No one would dream of doing anything of the sort. I do have a serious operation against the Corrigans under way, yes. But I would not have allowed any action finally to go forward without having fully put you in the picture.'

'Wouldn't you? I'm glad to hear it. So, come now. The details. All the details.'

'It's like this, sir. My informant told me, some time ago now, that the Corrigans had got wind of a large consignment of Class A drugs coming into Norchester airport for onward transmission to some criminal organization on the continent. They had conceived the notion of hijacking it. At that stage I did consider attempting to pinpoint the arrival of the import in question and seizing it ourselves. But eventually it seemed best to me, sir, not to risk a bungled operation. I thought we should wait till the Corrigans moved in. Then we could simultaneously seize the drug and arrest the Corrigans on a major charge.'

'What major charge, Mr French? I'm not sure that I understand.'

Asking all the right questions. The wrong questions.

'They would have been caught committing an armed robbery, sir.'

'Armed? Armed? And did you know that they were intending to use guns? Here? In Norchester?'

A quick glance at George Grundy. Would there be any back-up from him if the truth was fudged?

A stony face gave him an immediate answer.

'Yes, sir, I was aware that the Corrigans would be armed. I could have deduced it, in fact, from what I knew of their methods. But it had actually come to our notice that a London criminal with a record of gun use had been brought up here.'

'And I was not told of that? Mr French, this operation of yours is ended. As from this minute.'

Nothing to be said in face of that.

But, as George Grundy closed the door behind them, he turned to him.

'Before you go home I want a word with you.'

He did not bother going to his desk and seating himself.

'Grundy, I'm right, aren't I, in supposing all that was arranged between the Chief and yourself?'

'What do you mean, *arranged*?'

'I mean that, in direct opposition to my known wishes, you went to the Chief and told him what I had in mind for the Corrigans. What you thought, in your wisdom, was not the way they should be handled.'

'Well, I was right, wasn't I? The Chief certainly thought so.'

'I don't care a bugger what the Chief thinks or doesn't think. What I do care about is that you decided you knew best and went behind my back to play on that old

157

woman's fears of proper action and his bloody hopes of ending his days as Sir fucking Arnold. You sabotaged everything I've been working to achieve.'

'I considered it my duty. You had no right to carry on behind the Chief's back in that way.'

'Something any one of us has done often and often with a superior officer. And something, as you should bloody well have known, I was hardly going to go on doing once I was ready to put the whole business to him in a way he could be made to understand.'

'Oh, you'd have done that, would you? I saw no signs of it. Day after day you were going further and further towards starting a full-scale gunfight with the Corrigans. And what's more, involving me in it. A fully updated report, you asked for only this morning. Just because I didn't write anything down, it doesn't mean I haven't remembered your exact words. *Men, dispositions, weaponry, everything.* Well, that's not the way we work in Norchester, and it was high time you found that out.'

'And it's high time you found something out, Detective Chief Superintendent Grundy. It's time you learnt that being a good detective means doing something more than waddling about telling criminals not to be naughty. It means putting the scum behind bars, or flat out dead on the pavement if it comes to it. That's what detectives are meant to do. Protect the stupid man in the street. Whether he wants it or not. Whether or not the judges and the politicians who pay us give us the backing we deserve.'

'Sir, I will not stand here to be insulted. *Waddling about.* I—'

'You've no need to stand here one minute longer, Grundy. You're off the Corrigan case. As from this minute. Leave all the briefing material you've collected out there with Shirley, and don't you dare breathe one word of all this to that precious daughter-in-law of yours. In future just concern yourself with wiping the noses of poor imitation criminals like old Daddy Duffell. Understood?'

'Sir.'

So when just a few hours later Deborah arrived for the weekend he had no hesitation, sitting up beside her there in the bed eating some supper, in telling her at full length everything from the time he had first unexpectedly bumped into Peter Kitson in Norchester right up until the Big White Chief had issued his *No*. All very well to respect the obligation to confidentiality, but when certain boundaries had been passed, as after that feeble plot between George Grundy and the Chief they certainly had, then he felt free to vent his grievance to the full.

'But, Ned, should you have done that to your Chief Superintendent Grundy? I mean, I've never met him, but surely he can't be quite as hopeless and inefficient as you've made him out to be. After all, he has got to where he has, head of his force CID, and you can't do that without having some good qualities.'

'Oh, yes, you can. Or, rather, you can get to the top of the tree, at least in somewhere like Norchester, by having good qualities that have nothing to do with good police work.'

'Oh, come on, Ned. You're being totally uncompromising.'

'Well, that's what I ought to be. No, what I've said's true. In somewhere like Norchester what you need to take you to the top in the police is plenty of yes-sir, no-sirring. Even if it's disguised, as it is with bloody George Grundy, as bluff Northern directness. Does you no harm either if you're a pillar of the chapel. Plus you must be a stickler for the unimportant, like good admin, keeping the statistics up to date, and bullying convictions out of poor hard-working whores and semi-criminals with no guts to do more than pick a few pockets. Or, like Daddy

159

Duffell, break into nice homes and pinch the video.'

'But, Ned, be fair. You told me yourself that Daddy did more than break into homes. You said he specialized in tying up anybody he found inside. So he can't have been quite the inept criminal you paint him as.'

'Can't he? What did he ever do but tie up old ladies so they could free themselves inside half an hour? Pathetic. No difficulty in policing a place, if that's the worst kind of offender you're up against. But you're not. Not even in Norchester. And we certainly weren't once the Corrigans had set foot in the place.'

'Well, yes, I see what you mean when you talk about them. If half what you've said is true. I mean, it is certain, is it, that the one you called Farty did kill that poor old Daddy Duffell?'

'Okay, I haven't got hundred per cent proof, but, no, there's no doubt in my mind Farty was responsible for that. And, to do George Grundy credit, there was no doubt in his mind either. Even if it meant he wanted to let Marty and Barty know we were on to them just for the pleasure of pulling in Farty straight away.'

She sat there then in silence, her empty plate of take-away pizza on her lap.

'Ned,' she said at last, in a voice more tentative than he had yet heard from her. 'Look, it's none of my business, of course, and I'd be the first to admit I don't know all the facts. But are you sure you're right in ditching everything else in order to take the Corrigans at the moment they try to grab that load of cocaine? I mean, you know they'll be carrying guns, and you know, if I've got what you said right, that at least Barty Corrigan and that awful-sounding Lucy the Luger won't hesitate to use them. I mean, you're bound to be risking people's lives that way, even if it's no more than the Corrigans' lives.'

'Oh God, you're not going to start now? I've had enough of that from my lily-livered Chief. Telling me to call the whole operation off. Call it off. A chance like this. Well, I may do nothing about it for a day or two. But I'm not going to let him get away with that.'

'Well, all right. I dare say he's not as much of a fire-eater as you'd like. But I must say I think he's got a point. I mean, people being killed. Even if they are criminals, Grade A criminals. And it needn't be just them. People could get killed on your side, couldn't they? Jesus, Ned, you could be killed, you, if you're really going to take over from George Grundy.'

'I certainly am. And bloody glad to have the opportunity. I was cursing my life not long ago for being swaddled in absurd admin instead of going out there putting the scum where they belong. Well, now I've got the chance to do just that, and I'm taking it with both hands.'

'With both hands clutching a gun yourself? It'll be that, won't it?'

'Not clutching, if you don't mind. But holding in the approved grip. And not afraid to fire.'

'But how long is it since you've fired a gun? Have you ever fired one in anger, even?'

'Oh, yes, I've done that. I held a gun ticket when I was in the Met. And I've arranged to go on the range here on Monday, sharpen up the skills. Provided, that is, that I'm not out at Obelisk Hill before then.'

'And without having fired a gun ever since you've been up here? With characters like that dreadful Farty loosing off everywhere? Ned, I'm frightened for you.'

'Well, you'll hardly have to be if it's Farty doing the shooting. Ugly brute's too stupid to know which end of a gun's which.'

'But you said – which one of them was it? Marty or Barty? – you said one of them took Farty out to Obelisk Hill and made him practise.'

'It was Marty, clever sod Marty. But he was only doing that to give himself cover for looking out the lie of the land for when they hijack that load. No, don't you worry about me. If you've got to worry about anybody, worry about the Corrigans and Lucy Luzzatto.'

'But that's it, Ned. It's your attitude. You seem quite ready, more than ready, to kill those men in cold blood. But, however ruthless they are as criminals, they are human beings. They've a right to life.'

'Oh, yes. So they have. A right to life while they're not engaged in trying to take other people's. But once they begin that, in my book they lose any rights they might have had. A warning, yes. Any killing that does get done won't be precisely in cold blood. If you don't shout *Armed Police* before you fire you're in deep trouble with the lords and masters afterwards. And I'd even say it's fair enough there should be a warning. But if criminals are pointing guns and if that shout's been uttered, then anything they get is no more than what they deserve.'

Again she was silent.

He thought about getting up and fetching the thick, cream-oozing chocolatey slices of cake he'd got stashed away in the fridge. But something in the set of her shoulders told him this was not the moment.

'Ned,' she said at last, 'I know everything you've told me can be justified. I even suspect you'd shout that warning more than once if you could. But all the same, there's something in your whole way of looking at— At criminals that I don't quite like. I know they're bad. Evil, if you like. The worst of them, people perhaps like the Corrigans. But I still think they're deserving of more consideration than you give them.'

'I'd say we were back to Heather Jonas.'

'Well, all right, perhaps we are. But let me remind you, in the end you came to admit Heather wasn't the evil person you thought she was. You've got to show tolerance sometimes.'

His turn now not to speak. Wondering if he should

162

say what he had in mind to say. Whether, if he uttered the words, that whole crystal globe they had encircling them would shatter.

But in the end he did speak.

'No. It's wrong to show what you call tolerance. That's only soft-bellied weakness. All right maybe if you're dealing with ordinary everyday human beings. But wrong – wrong, wrong, wrong – if you're faced with criminals. If you're faced with scum like the Corrigans. *Don't give the buggers one inch.* I told you once that was my motto. Well, it is. And it always will be.'

Was the crystal splintered to pieces?

'The good detective,' she said. 'The good detective's creed.'

He was unable to make out whether it was said with reluctant admiration or concealed contempt.

The crystal trembling but intact. Just.

# 17

As soon as he had cleared the Monday morning junk from his desk he set off on his usual little trip to look in on the Collator.

'Morning, Inspector. So, what sort of a weekend has our friend Gismo Hawkins been having? Or has no officer of the Norchester Constabulary so much as set eyes on him?'

'Oh, yes, sir, one of them has. Report just come in. PC Sarah Weller. Yesterday evening while off duty she noticed our Gismo driving a bloody great laundry van, if you please. Suppose he's bought it for some more or less devious purpose.'

'Or stolen it, Inspector? That's his form, isn't it?'

'Well, yes, sir. Gismo's made off with more than one motor vehicle in his time, not that we've ever been able to prove it.'

'But never before a big van? Or am I wrong?'

'Well, yes, sir, this does seem to be a bit of a departure. My experience of Gismo anyhow.'

'Right. PC Weller tell you the name on the van by any chance?'

'Yes, sir. She did as a matter of fact. The White Eagle Laundry.'

'Good work. Check with the laundry that they've got a vehicle missing, will you? I'd be surprised if they haven't.'

He went back to his office almost at a run, snatched

up the phone and spoke to Inspector Oxford, in charge of the Armed Response team.

'Gismo Hawkins, who works for the Corrigans nowadays, has just stolen a large van. White Eagle Laundry. You know, *Eagle Eyed for Spots and Specks*. There's lots of them around. Pound to a penny it's what they intend to use out at Obelisk Hill. To block the vehicle with the stuff in it.'

'So it'll be any time now, sir?'

'It will. Your chaps all ready?'

'Yes, sir. Full muster this morning.'

'Good man.'

'When will Mr Grundy be doing the briefing, sir?'

'He won't be. I'm running this myself. I'll let you know when I'm ready for briefing.'

'Right, sir.'

But plain enough there was a query Oxford would have liked to put. If he had known how.

'Well, sir, we'll be very glad to have you out there with us.'

'I hope you will be, Inspector. Though not everyone may be all that keen to have an Assistant Chief at their elbow.'

'Know what you mean, sir. But I think my lads'll welcome it.'

'We'll see, Inspector. In the meanwhile let them know it could be tomorrow or the day after. At the latest. And tell them to keep their damn mouths shut.'

No sooner had he put the phone down when Shirley rang through.

'It's Norchester airport. Head of security.'

'Yes? Hello there. What've we got?'

'Cargo aircraft just landed. I've seen the waybill. Green beans. This could be the consignment you wanted to know about.'

'So it could. You have any idea how long crates like that are kept in store?'

'I've only just heard this lot's arrived. I'll make inquiries. Could be only a matter of hours, or they could stay with us the best part of a week. But they don't generally stay here that long.'

He felt the blood running with all the vigour of his days in the Met when a major operation was at launch point.

But before this particular operation there was one last obstacle to be jumped over, knocked down or slid round.

Off to see the Big White Chief.

'Yes, Mr French?'

Guarded hostility written all over the face with the misleadingly bristling eyebrows.

'A quick word, sir, if I might?'

'Not about that Corrigan business, I trust. I hope I made myself perfectly clear about that last week.'

'You did, sir. But it is about the Corrigans.'

A glare of sharply defensive hostility. Bad sign. And good. Manic determination not to allow his force to be involved in something that could result in the least sniff of bad publicity. But, equally, the gnawing inner knowledge that in failing to fight crime to the bitter end he was not doing what it was his duty to do.

'I'll make no bones about it, sir, I've come to persuade you to take a different view.'

'Mr French, my mind is made up. Finally.'

'With respect, sir, I wonder if you have altogether appreciated the full seriousness of what it is the Corrigans are doing. Sir, my information is that the consignment of drugs they're planning to seize is as large as any that has come into this country. Possibly the largest ever.'

Sharp forward jerk across the wide polished surface of the desk.

'Ah, but, Mr French, what's the true strength of that information? Does it come from that nark of yours, now in hospital? I'd be much inclined to doubt anything from

166

a source of that sort. He'd have nothing to lose by whatever gross exaggeration he cared to employ.'

'Very true, sir. You know the sort of person most snouts are, as well or better than any of us I dare say.'

Flattery visibly going down nicely as an after-dinner mint. Press on.

'But I think if you'd had the chance to meet my man before his accident, you'd look on him in a different light. The truth of the matter is, sir, that I had him tamed right down to the last piece of gristle in his whole slithery body. He's been running scared with me, sir, long before the Corrigans brought him up to Norchester. He couldn't spin me a lie however much good it'd do him.'

'Well, if you say so . . .'

'I do, sir. So the fact remains that we're dealing here with what may well turn out to be as big an act of criminality as we'll see anywhere in the whole country this year. Or for many years to come.'

If Peter was running scared, it'll be nothing to the way I'm going to get this superannuated old lady going.

'Mr French, don't please think I underrate the gravity of the Corrigans' invasion of Norchester. Though I'm bound to add that I don't think you made out as serious a case as this against them previously. However, let that pass . . .'

'Yes, sir. But I hope you do see now that it's been necessary to mount an operation on a scale that will put paid to their activities once and for all.'

'Mr French, please don't think I've been in any way— In any way— Well, dragging my heels in the matter. It's just that I felt I was not being allowed to exercise my responsibilities to the full. No doubt you had your reasons. But I must say I feel you should have trusted me. To— To come up with the right response. Yes, the right response.'

'I'm sorry if you felt that, sir. I promise you that was not at all my intention. Any more than it ever was to try and say the steps I've taken towards a final confrontation with the Corrigans had gone too far to be stopped. You have my assurance you would have been told exactly what was going to happen before that point was reached. But I thought it necessary to exercise maximum security. Whatever you may have been told about the Corrigans, sir, the fact is there's a lot more to them than a family of ne'er-do-wells who just need to be pushed out beyond the city boundaries.'

'I've certainly never thought that, Mr French. Never.'

Except when you were listening to fat and satisfied Detective Chief Superintendent George Grundy, you prize touch for any sort of soft soap.

'You're perfectly right, sir. These are evil men. At any cost they ought to be locked up long enough to stop them doing harm for years to come. I'd even go so far as to say they ought to be strung up, all three of them.'

Behind the wide desk a shuffling movement of anxious protest.

Take advantage. Let him off Hook A: secure him past all wriggling on Hook B.

'Mr French...'

'But that's a matter I'm entirely prepared to accept your judgment on, sir.'

'Very well.'

Good. Another nail rammed home. Bang in again.

'The point I'd like to make now, sir, is that the Corrigans in coming up here, invading Norchester if you like, have actually seriously over-extended themselves. They're attempting to go for much bigger stakes than they ever have before. So at just this moment, because they are over-extended, they're weak. Ready for the chop.'

And at the word *weak* another degree of relief visible. The weak able to be beaten, hopefully.

'But on the other hand, sir, if we don't act to deal with them at once and effectively, our responsibility will be enormous.'

168

And it was plain he had found the final telling argument. Responsibility for a failure. Not to be thought of. Not for the future Sir Arnold. Especially if, without too many risks, it could be avoided.

Pounce.

'If by some chance it became known to the media, sir, that an opportunity to eliminate as serious a threat to society as we've seen for many a year had been wilfully missed – and one could never guarantee the facts wouldn't leak out one way or another – then we each of us could expect to live out the rest of our careers under a densely black cloud.'

Across the desk a look of grave thoughtfulness. Fuelled, no doubt, by the recollection that a former senior Met detective was not unlikely to have contacts among the London crime reporters.

'Well, Mr French, I take note of your arguments. I can promise you I shall give the whole matter my full consideration. And in the meanwhile I suppose you had better carry on. But—' A last splutter of bristling fierceness. 'But let me make it totally clear. Nothing irrevocable is to be done before I have been fully informed. Is that understood?'

'Absolutely understood, sir.'

Understood in all its underlying meaning. A quick memo just as the Armed Response team leave to take up their places, and honour will be satisfied. Responsibility without complications.


Another call from the airport head of security.

'That consignment, Mr French. Now safely stowed in one of our refrigerated sheds. But no indication so far as to when it's to be collected.'

'So we may have to wait a little yet?'

'I suppose you will. But, Mr French, there is one thing. I know you like to keep security tight, but all the same can't you tell me just what is it in fact we're sitting on? I mean, unless you know something to the contrary, this could be no more than a lot of innocent green beans. Do you want me to go and take a peek?'

'No. No, absolutely not. I've had, in fact, a good indication that load's going to be on the move before very long, and I don't want the least suspicion aroused. There may well be people up at your end, in and around that particular area even, who'd be quick enough to pass out a message. So behave strictly as normal. All right?'

'All right, will do.'

Then another incoming call. An altogether unexpected one.

'Ned? Ned? It's me, Deborah.'

'Oh, hi. Nice surprise. You thinking of coming up before the weekend? Only, it's not really a very good—'

'No, Ned, no. Listen, have you got anybody with you? Is it all right to say something? Something important?'

'Yes, I suppose so. I've certainly got no one with me. But, well, just occasionally switchboards have ears. But what is it? Can't be anything too serious. Or can it be?'

'Yes, Ned, it is serious. Very. But I'll try to keep it to a minimum.'

'What are you going to tell me, for heaven's sake?'

'It's this. A friend of yours— Well, someone you once told me was no friend of yours actually... Know who I mean?'

Suddenly filled with mind-racing foreboding, he had the sense on the open line not to say aloud the words *Palmy Palmer.*

'Yes, all right. But he's not been in touch with you, has he? I'll bloody murder him if—'

'No, no. It's— It's something I've just heard about him. I— Well, I was round at— His place of work, yes. There. Making some inquiries about a client. Okay? And— And— I happened to hear that he, this guy, is in bad trouble.'

'Trouble? What sort of trouble?'

170

'I don't know exactly. I didn't like to ask too many questions, not about someone I'm hardly supposed to know. But this was the gossip.'

'What gossip? Exactly?'

'That he had been— Suspended.'

The word shot out in a single quick breath.

But he had heard enough.

'I see. And you think it's because of, shall we say, something long ago?'

'Well, it could hardly be anything else, could it?'

'Oh, it could be, knowing our friend. Or not-friend. But, yes, it certainly might be what you think. Yes.'

'But, Ned, what are you going to do, if it is what I think it is? What I'm afraid it might be?'

'Good question.'

He thought rapidly. A juggling of times and expectations.

'Ned?'

If the load of green beans began its journey as soon as it looked likely, it should still be all right. Whatever was happening in Nottingham. It would take time to get Palmy to talk. Or, even if Palmy, paranoid about being shat on from above, produced that statement, those three little forgeries, almost at once, there would still be time. Time enough to put the Corrigans out of account once and for all.

After that to hell with everything.

'Look, love, I can't speak now. Not for a dozen good reasons. But I— I'll phone when I can, though that may not be for some while. Things a bit hairy up here.'

'Hairy?'

'Nothing to worry about.'

'But, Ned, I do worry.'

'I know you do. And— And, well, it's been a long time since anybody's worried about me. So I'm grateful. More than, as a matter of fact.'

'But, Ned—'

171

'No, sweetheart. And about what you rang me over. For the moment there's nothing I can do. And by the time there is – though I don't at this instant see what I can do in any case – by the time there is it may turn out to have been nothing to do with me. Yes?'

'Oh God, Ned, I hope so.'

'Well, thank you for that. And— Look, I think I'd better ring off now. I'll be in touch when I can. Promise.'

'Please. Yes, please. And I love you, you know.'

'Yes, I know. Reciprocated, as a matter of fact. So I really hope, too, it's not what you think. However . . .'

'Yes, however. Well, goodbye then. Goodbye.'

''bye.'

# 18

He had arranged the briefing for two o'clock. With no tip from the airport that the green beans consignment had been booked out there was little chance of it starting its journey south at once. But the Armed Response team ought to be a hundred per cent ready. So a little time to familiarize himself with Grundy's preparations and no doubt to make a few changes. Then an hour or so out at the force range. Get his hand in.

As far as the team on obbo at the Corrigans' house had been able to make out, Marty and Barty were safely indoors there. Equally, the 'manageress' at the Silver Street launderette had reported Farty and Lucy the Luger still installed in the flat above. A little time, at least, in hand.

If none to think what Palmy's suspension might mean. Nothing like furious activity to thrust aside awkward dilemmas.

So at ten minutes to two he was waiting in the Parade Room for the arrival of the marksmen. A large-scale map of Parbrook Forest was pinned on the wall behind him. Photographs of the three Corrigans, Lucy the Luger and Gismo Hawkins, mug shots and full-length, were fixed beside it. A semi-circle of folding wooden chairs faced him.

There was a knock at the door and a cadet came in.

'I was told to bring this to you here, sir.'

He took the proffered envelope, opened it and found

what he had asked the force photographic unit to get, a picture of a White Eagle Laundry van, twin of the one Gismo Hawkins had stolen. *Eagle Eyed for Spots and Specks.*

'Right, lad. Pin this up beside that map.'

Before the cadet had finished the team came in. He waited until the cadet had scurried away and then turned to the men seated in front of him.

'Good afternoon, gentlemen. I don't know whether Inspector Oxford has told you who I am. But, in case any of you don't know me, I'm Assistant Chief Constable French, and I shall be personally directing the operation you are going on. In the field. So make sure you'll be able to recognize me under any circumstances. I don't much fancy being on the receiving end of a bullet from any one of you.'

A murmur of laughter. The boss having his little joke.

'Equally, gentlemen, I have no particular wish to put a bullet into any of you. So you will oblige me by standing up in turn and giving me your names while I take a good look at you. Inspector Oxford I know well enough. But I'm not sure I have met all of you. So, begin at the back on the left, please.'

He looked over to where the first man in the team was rising to his feet. And recognized someone he did know, if not all that well.

'Detective Constable Tucker, sir.'

Terry Tucker, CID romeo, lover of George Grundy's daughter-in-law Cindy.

While the fellow stood there, grinning round, making a bit of a show of himself, he thought quickly.

Would Cindy have confided to him she was being blackmailed by whatever go-between Marty Corrigan had used? Told him she was feeding out information from her father-in-law's old envelopes and odd pieces of paper? Probably not. Tell this known bed-hopper their affair had led her into dangerously bad trouble, and, she must know, he was more than likely to drop her like a pan hot off the stove.

Nor did Tucker, standing there looking him straight in the face now, exuding male pride, have any air of having a secret to hide. So make no trouble. Let him stay.

'All right, next if you please.'

One by one the rest of the team stood up and identified themselves.

'Right then, let's hope there'll be no unpleasant mistakes. Because, believe you me, gentlemen, there's every chance of the possibility arising. Operations of this sort never, repeat never, go according to plan.'

He looked round to make sure the point had sunk in.

'And that brings me to the next thing. You're all trained for the job in hand. Well trained, I trust. You've all been told a hundred and one times that you will draw your handgun from its holster only if you believe, with reason, that a life is threatened. You all have been told time and again that, if you do have occasion to draw your weapon, you are not to fire unless there's been a shout of *Armed Police*. But, let me remind you, that warning may be as much for the benefit of one of your colleagues as for the criminal scum who are threatening to shoot. Things can go wrong, gentlemen. Particularly in an operation out in the depths of the country. If we have the villains we're hoping to collar surrounded, then some of you are likely to be directly facing others. So, take this for real. Not a shot till that shout *Armed Police* has been loudly and clearly given. Understood?'

Again he looked round the semi-circle of marksmen. And made sure he had a nod of agreement from each one of them.

'Now, gentlemen, let me put you fully in the picture about the operation itself. Not only about what will be expected of you when we ambush the ambushers of what may well prove to be the largest consignment of cocaine ever brought into this country, but about the men we'll

175

be going up against. Criminals I've had the doubtful pleasure of having dealings with during my time in the Met. Again, the more you know of them the less chance there is of things going wrong.'

He turned to the photos on the wall beside the map.

'First, Barty Corrigan, Bartholomew Corrigan, aged forty-two, previous convictions for grievous bodily harm, armed robbery and half a dozen other offences. A man who will stop at nothing. Who will do whatever it takes to get what he wants. No great brain. But one hell of a lot of willpower. A dangerous man, gentlemen. When I've finished, go and take a good, long look at his photo. It may be a matter of life and death. For you.'

Over to Marty Corrigan's picture.

'Martin Corrigan, aged forty-one, cousin of Barty, known as Marty. No convictions. Note that, gentlemen, no convictions. Why? Because he's been too damn clever. Until now. He's perfectly capable, let me warn you, of infiltrating this force, by blackmail, intimidation, bribery, whatever it takes.'

He contrived a quick glance at DC Tucker. And saw no particular emotion on his face.

'So, watch your tongues. I hope it won't be very long, possibly not many hours, before we go in against these people. But don't let me ever find that, during that waiting period, any one of you has been boasting or hinting or making yourself into a glamour boy by saying anything at all about what you have heard or are going to hear in this room this afternoon.'

And on to Farty Corrigan's thick-necked likeness.

'Francis Corrigan, aged thirty-five. Known, for obvious reasons, as Farty. Almost certainly the murderer of one Daddy Duffell, old Norchester small-time criminal. A brute. An ignorant brute. But a damn dangerous one. We've reason to believe he'll be carrying. And from my previous knowledge of him I can tell you he'll have very little idea who or what he's shooting at. So make sure you don't get in the way. And if it falls to you eventually to put handcuffs on him, watch yourself till they finally click into place. And then still watch.'

Another move along the picture gallery.

'Mario Luzzatto, known as Lucy the Luger. Two convictions for armed robbery. Reputed to be very fast on the draw and a considerable marksman with that favoured weapon of his. Homosexual. But don't for one moment fall into the trap of thinking he's some sort of a softie. Do that and you'll end up in a long box with a procession of officers in uniform marching at slow pace behind you.'

And the final photograph.

'Gismo Hawkins, probably better known to most of you than he is to me. I have reason to believe he will be driving a stolen White Eagle Laundry van, photo here. *Eagle Eyed for Spots and Specks.*'

A ripple of laughter. With underneath a hint of nervousness.

Pick up the pointer, tap its end on the map at the Obelisk Hill crossroads.

'The van's first purpose will be to block the path of a vehicle on its way to the south, and eventually the continent, with a consignment of produce from Latin America, prominently labelled *Green Beans*. In fact cocaine. The Corrigan mob probably intend to drive away with the loot in the van. It is my intention, however, to intervene just as the Corrigans make their bid and arrest all the participants. Whatever resistance they may offer.'

He turned back to the semi-circle of keenly attentive faces.

'Now, possible complications. So far as we have been able to make out the so-called owners of this consignment have not sent any minders to Norchester to look after the load on its journey. And, judging by the fact that the Corrigans are fielding only a team of four, or five if you count the driver, Hawkins, they may well have information that no protection is being provided. However, we may have failed to spot any such minders, or, if the goods are not going to start on their journey immediately, the minders may not have arrived. But you will understand the possibilities for confusion if we find ourselves in some sort of three-handed fire-fight. The prime one being that one of you gentlemen will shoot another.'

A sort of laugh.

'So the utmost vigilance and quickness of response, please. At the range you'll have all gone through the drill of either shooting or holding your fire according to what dummy target comes up. Well, here's your chance to show you've learnt your lessons.'

He looked at the faces in front of him. They appeared to have taken in what he had said.

'Right. Now Inspector Oxford will show you on the map here where each one of you will lie in wait as that load approaches Obelisk Hill crossroads. There, in the clough on the road leading up the hill, Gismo Hawkins and his laundry van will, I believe, be waiting. Judging by the fact that up to this moment Marty and Barty are in their house at the South End and Farty and Lucy are still in a flat we have under surveillance in Pratts Town, I fully expect the modus operandi will be to follow the load at a discreet distance in a fast car. Near the crossroads they will close in on the driver and his mate, and possibly any escorting villains, just as Gismo and his van block the road. No doubt Gismo will be equipped with a mobile phone and be maintaining contact.'

One more look round the semi-circle.

'Right. Then, finally, I myself will be in a car stationed some distance further along the road through the forest. I will advance to the scene of action as soon as I get a message that the ambush is taking place. Now, any questions?'

Questions came. By the dozen. Sharp and excited. He dealt with them and handed over to Inspector Oxford.

Listening to him explain where each man of the team was to hide, he could not stop himself wondering whether the plan would work.

But he stamped down the doubts.

It would work. He had done everything necessary. This was what he had been trained to do. From the moment he had joined the service, really. It was what he had trained himself for. From the day he had put into words in his head that motto, *Don't give the buggers one inch.* From the moment he had realized what his true ambition was: to be a good detective.

Just that.

And now, now he had reached what well might be the peak of the career he had pledged himself to. The good detective had done everything a good detective should have done, faced with the volcano threat that the Corrigans were. The good detective was ready to reap his harvest.

Harvest of evil.

He was in his office an hour and more earlier than usual next morning. Was this going to be the day? In all likelihood, yes.

The door opened. George Grundy. Face set in a mask of stiffness. An almost military manner even in turning to push the door closed again.

'Good morning, sir.'

'Well, what can I do for you?'

He felt a tiny zinging of impatience. What in God's name could the fellow be wanting now? Today? The day?

'There's something it's my duty to report.'

'Oh, yes?'

'It seems you never informed the team I put to watching the Corrigan house that I was no longer in charge of the operation.'

179

'No. No. I suppose I didn't. My fault.'

'Be that as it may. My men there have reported something very interesting.'

'Well?'

'The Corrigans, all three of them plus Lucy Luzzatto, have just left the house on their way back to London.'

'They were seen to go? You're sure? Your team there are certain?'

'Oh, yes. Farty came back to the house from the flat in Silver Street, with Luzzatto, late last night. When my WDC in the launderette wasn't, of course, still there to see them go. However, they were spotted entering the South End house at 12.25 a.m. That's this morning, Tuesday.'

'And you say all three of them, all four of them, have left now? For London? How did your team there know that?'

'Very simple. The Corrigans have gone down by train. My boys had the sense to follow their car when they saw all four targets leaving the house. They watched them put their vehicle in the railway car park and enter the station. So they simply asked the booking clerk where they'd taken tickets to, and the answer was *Four first-class to London*. Looks like the whole affair's off.'

A wonderfully smug look of triumph on the solid, ruddy-complexioned face.

# 19

Ned took a moment to make up his mind whether or not to stub out that smug look. The wishful thinking. Answer: not.

'Thank you, George. I'll act accordingly.'

No sooner had his door closed – a gesture of exaggerated care – than he grabbed his phone, tapped out Inspector Oxford's number.

'Oxford? Mr French here.'

'Sir?'

'Listen, the Corrigans and Lucy the Luger took a train for London first thing this morning. With, I gather, maximum ostentation. No doubt Marty Corrigan's arranged some nice respectable, bloody lying alibi for them all down there. So I reckon today must be the day. What's the first stop on the line south from here?'

'Micklebury Junction, sir. If the train's not a local.'

'Right. And that's about how far away? Travelling time?'

'Just over an hour.'

'So they could be on their way back any minute now in whatever zippy car Gismo Hawkins or someone's stolen for them and left at Micklebury. Then it'll be shadowing that load of so-called green beans as it leaves the airport transit sheds, all ready to go for it as soon as it gets well into Parbrook Forest. You'd better get your chaps out to Obelisk Hill at once. I'll be on my way myself, just as soon as I've drawn a weapon. Send whoever you've allocated as my driver down to the garage. I'll have my car waiting.'

'Right, sir. Good oh.'

It was only when he entered the garage some fifteen minutes later, standard issue .38 in its holster at his side, a memo to the Chief Constable being typed up by Shirley for onward transmission, that he saw who it was Inspector Oxford had chosen to drive him. Detective Constable Terry Tucker.

For an instant he thought about sending him away. But too late now for him to replace any of the marksmen already on their way out to the crossroads. And in any case why shouldn't Tucker come? After all, he'd done nothing wrong in itself. It had only been stupidly risky of him to have started an affair with the wife of Detective Chief Superintendent Grundy's son, Grundy with absolute zero tolerance for sexual irregularities of any sort. But no doubt the lad would pay for that error, one way or another, after the business ahead was over and it was safe to give Cindy Grundy what she deserved.

'It's Terry, isn't it? Hop in and we'll be on our way. Sort out a few prize villains. Lovely day for it.'

'Can't wait, sir.'

Actually bouncing on his toes.

But they did have to wait. They had left Headquarters at just after ten. They arrived at the place he had fixed on to station his vehicle at ten-forty, after taking a round-about way so as to be sure of not meeting the Corrigans' car driving up from Micklebury on its way to the airport a few miles further north. Eleven o'clock came and went. Half-past eleven. Twelve.

He would have liked to use the radio to find out what, if anything, was happening. But he had ordered strict radio silence until the final messages, *Cargo leaving* and then *Approaching area* and finally *In, in, in.*

182

Half-past twelve. One. Half-past.

His few attempts at conversation with Terry Tucker had long ago petered out. They sat instead in uneasy calm. Only the noise of Tucker tap-tap-tapping on the steering wheel in front of him broke the silence, bar through the car's lowered windows the hum of insect life in the warm May sunshine and the more distant rising and falling twitter of birds.

Now he could no longer prevent the news he had had from Deborah fully erupting into his consciousness. For the whole of the evening before he had managed to thrust it to the back of his mind, not without the aid of whisky. He had not even allowed it to keep him awake when he had tumbled into bed. In so far as anything had kept him from sleep it had been last, niggling, unnecessary ideas about how the ambush would go.

But now, waiting and waiting with nothing more to be done whatever extra precautions it might have been worth adding – and there were none – the thought of Palmy Palmer under suspension buzzed and darted in his mind like a trapped wasp.

What offence had Palmy actually been suspended for? With someone like him it could be a hundred and one things. He was certainly not above taking a bribe. Dozens of criminals over the years must have asked him that old sideways question, *Is there, you know, anything that can be done?* And received the nod in return. It was very probable he had in his time done what Cindy Grundy had done too, fed information to some gang leader. In his case more likely for money than under pressure. Even back in the days when they had been in the same CID room he had been notorious for improving his arrest record, where he could, by planting the odd piece of evidence or by verballing any petty thief stupid enough not to deny saying more than he had. Some more recent exploit of that sort might have caught up with him.

If only it was that ... But how much more likely it was that, with the waves Deborah had made or the attention that the *Justice Watch* programme had brought, it was something arising from the Heather Jonas business that had finally tripped him up.

So in a few days' time would whatever Palmy might say in his attempts to wriggle out of any blame come crashing down on his own head?

And then what?

Suspension himself, of course. Long interviews with an officer working under the Police Complaints Authority. And, almost for a certainty, the end of his career. No final post as a chief anywhere. Retirement. Idle days. If not worse.

But do I really want to be a chief? I used to think I did. Without ever much considering what it would be like. But it used to seem to be the reward for the years of putting criminals away. Yet now I know what it'd be. All the stupid admin and paper-pushing I have now, times ten. Fart-arsing about telling lies for the good name of whatever force I found myself heading. Becoming a copy of the future Sir Arnold.

No, damn it all, that's not what being a detective is.

So if this is to be the peak of it all, putting the Corrigans and scum like Lucy the Luger into the net, well, it may be not such a bad ending.

Christ, but it's hot in here. Bloody Tucker's sweating like a pig now. Worse really than the heat warrants. Nerves getting at him?

What about mine?

Careful body check.

No. Sweat no more than it ought to be. Heart rate normal. Muscles relaxed. After all, this is something I've done more than a few times.

But when's it going to begin?

Damn it, have they even been able to spot Gismo Hawkins and his laundry van hidden there in the clough?

God knows. He may not be there at all. This may not be the day, despite the Corrigans poncing off on that London train.

Have I got it all wrong? Was bloody George Grundy right? Corrigans got cold feet? Gone, tail between legs, back to the Smoke? Oh, come on, is it likely—

*Cargo leaving.* The open radio channel had crackled into life, and then there had come those two swift words.

'Right. Shouldn't be long now, Terry. We reckoned it'll take an HGV fifteen or twenty minutes to reach the crossroads.'

'Going to be a heavy goods truck, is it, then, sir? We know that, do we?'

'No, we don't. Not for a fact. But the stuff it's going to be bringing won't fit in a suitcase, not by a long chalk.'

'They never gave us its number or description on the radio. Stupid bastards.'

'My orders. No point in keeping radio to a minimum if we're going to put out the number of the vehicle the Corrigans are following for them to pick up. These are not children we're dealing with.'

'If they are following it, sir.'

A mutinous murmur.

Yes, nerves. Have to think again about having this one in the Armed Response team. If George Grundy doesn't succeed in getting rid of him altogether.

They fell silent.

Now the tension was beginning to get to him too. Still, no bad thing. Not at this time when—

*Approaching area*

Tucker's hand felt at his holster.

'Leave that alone, man. Until you see a life threatened. Right?'

'Always thought that was just for the media, sir.'

'Well, it's not. Christ, didn't you listen to a word I said yesterday?'

Definitely off the team.

*In, in, in*
'Right, put your foot down.'

It was much as he had expected. A tall old van, *White Eagle Laundry*, squarely across the tarmac just where the turning down to the clough came up into the main road. A big container vehicle with its nose almost touching the van's side. Behind, a powerful BMW slewed across the road some ten yards back.

Five figures, heads hidden in khaki balaclavas, at the container truck's cab. Guns in the hands of four of them. From various points around, the Armed Response lads surfacing. Someone – Inspector Oxford? – shouting again and again through a loudhailer, 'Armed Police. Armed Police. Put down your guns. We have you surrounded. Put down your weapons.'

Tucker had brought the car to a screeching halt. They flung the doors open. Tumbled out.

Then, just as they emerged, there came the sound of shots. Three or four in quick succession. One of the police team, in poor cover, fell to the ground just beyond the road. The four of them with the guns made a break for the gap in the cordon.

And – bloody hell – there, where they were heading for, some two hundred yards along the road on the opposite side from the clough was a battered old Morris estate, pulled in on the verge. With a family, man, wife, two kids, just putting picnic things in at its rear doors. Baskets, folding chairs, rugs. A little black-and-white dog was jumping up at them. None of them, seemingly, taking any notice of the shots that had banged out any more than if it had been someone with a shotgun out after rabbits.

One of the Corrigans, Barty or Marty, must have spotted the Morris. An escape vehicle.

Or, doubly bad scenario, seen the civilians as hostages. Specks and spots on the burnished plans. Worse.

The three Corrigans and the hooded figure who must be Lucy Luzzatto were charging away down the road now. Gismo Hawkins, still by the container truck, had his hands up resting on top of his balaclava-covered head.

With Tucker he himself was easily the nearest to the four of them making for the Morris estate.

He put his head down and ran, pulling his pistol from his holster. Lives were in danger.

'This way, Tucker, this way,' he yelled into the air.

He thought he heard Tucker's steps pounding on the road behind.

The Corrigans seemed not to have realized how close the two of them were.

Fire? No, no, no. This range anything could happen.

The family with the picnic had caught on to what was happening at last. Father, mother, the two little girls in gingham dresses, one yellow, one pink, frozen there. The dog suddenly crouching silent.

Tucker had drawn level with him. He was raising his gun.

He wouldn't be such a—

Too late. The crack of his .38.

Idiot.

And the sole result, the Corrigans wheeling round.

For a moment, for half a minute, the four balaclava-ringed faces confronted them. Thirty yards distant, thirty-five. Guns swinging up.

'Down,' he yelled to Tucker. 'Down, man.'

He flung himself to the ground, propped himself on his elbows, levelled his pistol.

'Farty, stay here. And you, Marty. Keep those fuckers where they are.'

It was Barty's voice. Easily heard. Hoarse with determination.

'Lucy, come on. We'll get the car. Grab the woman.'

He took a swift glance back to see how near Oxford and his men were.

Coming up. But not near enough.

'Right, Tucker,' he said quietly. 'When you see me go, on your feet.'

He allowed himself two deep breaths.

And up.

Shot after shot from in front.

But Farty firing. Gun jerking about like a live thing.

From just behind him Tucker fired now.

Marty, just dropping into a solid shooting stance, keeled over and fell.

Good man. Knew which to go for.

And Farty turning tail, lumbering off. But at a pace.

Down by the car Barty and Lucy, each clearly recognizable now, had acted quickly enough. Lucy stood beside the car, his gun pointing at father and children. Barty had the mother by the arm and had begun to push her into the vehicle through its wide open rear doors.

'Tucker, hold back,' he shouted himself.

For a moment it looked as if his order was being deliberately not heard. Tucker took a pace or two forward, ready to run.

'Tucker. Stay where you are.'

It stopped him.

He looked behind again. Oxford and almost all the rest of the team were coming up fast.

'Come with me, Tucker,' he called over. 'I'm going to get round the far side of them if I can.'

'Right, sir.'

At least the fellow was accepting orders now.

Ahead the road took a sharp curve to the left. It ought to be possible to cut across to somewhere on the far side of the car. Unless Barty got the woman into it pretty quickly. And she was resisting.

'The children. Children.'

Her voice, shrill with fear, came to him. And her struggles, senseless though they were, were fully occupying Barty.

188

And would go on doing so. Unless his patience snapped and he dealt with her. One way or another.

He ran forward hard along the road, Tucker at his heels.

Just before they reached an easy place to get up on to the heathery moorland they found Marty lying half on the roadway, half on the verge. Leg twisted under him and a heavy patch of blood darkening the trousers of his flashy Prince-of-Wales suit. From the stillness of his body it looked as if he must be more or less unconscious. But his gun was still in his hand.

On the run, he stooped, caught the weapon up and flung it as far as he could into the tussocky heather.

Nice job for some cadets tomorrow. Find it and preserve the evidence.

Up off the road.

The going through the pinky-purple carpet of heather was hard. Worse than he had counted on. Like trying to run on an immense bouncy cushion.

Could the two of them make it to the far side of the escape car before Barty got away?

He risked a quick look over his shoulder.

And, bonus. Farty had arrived at the car and seemed at once to have begun a shouted argument with his cousin.

He halted for a moment – bliss to catch his breath – letting Tucker plunge on ahead and tried to make out what was happening.

'Bloody poofter.'

Farty's shout came clearly to him. Was he wanting Lucy to mow down the whole family there under his gun? God knows.

Now Lucy turned and yelled something indistinguishable in Farty's direction, raising his gun. Barty shouted something at the pair of them, and, as he did so, the mother broke from his grasp and ran staggeringly towards her daughters.

Thieves fall out. But not necessarily enough.

Without risking waiting to see the outcome, he set off across the heather again.

Tucker was some twenty or thirty yards ahead, and it looked as if he at least would reach the road again before Barty could turn the escape car and come up.

Would Tucker, damn hothead, try shooting at its tyres at full range? Dangerous. And totally forbidden. Endless investigations afterwards, whatever way it all went.

He put his head down and forced himself to run yet faster, bouncing and swerving. Sick with effort.

The road again at last. Tucker standing there, gun held in front of him in the classic two-handed grip.

'Right, Tucker,' he gasped. 'But not a shot till I give word.'

'Sir, I could cripple that estate with one round.'

'Listen to orders, damn you.'

'Sir.'

Gun ostentatiously lowered.

From the far side there came now the sound of Inspector Oxford's loud-hailer.

'Mr French, I see you in place. Mr French, I see you. Barty Corrigan, you are surrounded again. Be sensible. You cannot escape. Throw down your guns, all three of you, and lie flat on the ground. I repeat, you cannot escape. Throw down your weapons.'

But already, it seemed, Barty had dealt with the spat between Farty and Lucy Luzzatto. Lucy was back menacing the father, who in fact had never shown much sign of needing menacing. Farty was clambering into the car's driving seat. Barty himself had run over and hauled back his hostage.

Pushing and shoving in no gentle manner he got her across the threshold into the back of the vehicle. Then he turned.

'I've got a hostage,' he shouted, his voice thinned in the wide open. 'I warn you, French, I won't hesitate to shoot her if you make me. You know me, even if these

190

bumpkins don't. So tell them to step back. We're going the other way, up to the crossroads and then south. If anyone tries to stop us it'll be the worse for the woman. Right?'

He was about to call out in answer, ceding to Barty's terms. Nothing else to be done.

But then just as Barty, gun in fist, began to scramble in beside his hostage, the little black-and-white dog, until that moment cowed as its master, for some unknown reason launched itself.

Its teeth sank into Barty's outstretched leg. He turned, struck at the beast with his gun, cursing, yelling.

They were not much more than fifty yards away. Ned hurled himself forward.

Ten seconds were all he needed. Less.

He had his gun rammed into Barty's face while the fellow's blows at the dog were still raining down.

'That's enough.'

He reached forward, tugged the gun from Barty's hand. A heavy Smith and Wesson.

Tucker, thank Christ, had cottoned on. He was already at the far side of the car now, hauling Farty out.

'Fucking idiots. Fucking idiots. Why did I ever come here?'

Lucy Luzzatto knew when he was beaten. He tore off his balaclava, threw down his gun.

The picnic party, now the danger was over, absurdly took to their heels and ran off along the road, mother and father each hauling along a child by one hand, dog playfully jumping up at them.

He let them run. If they felt happier that way . . .

Oxford and his men came up. In a minute Barty and Lucy were safely handcuffed. From the far side of the car Tucker came round, his gun firmly jammed in Farty's back.

'One more for the bus to nowhere,' he said with irrepressible cheerfulness.

191

And at that moment Farty threw himself backwards with his whole lardy weight. Tucker went down. Farty, with more speed than seemed possible, rolled round, grabbed Tucker's gun and heaved himself to his feet.

No one had the presence of mind to stop him. In seconds he was off down the road in the same direction as the fleeing picnickers.

It was almost comical.

Until the sound of shots – one, two, three – blasted out.

Farty, mad with rage or totally confused, was loosing off at the civilians. Or in that vague direction.

Lives in danger?

Ned did not stop to weigh the fine points.

He dropped to one knee, lifted his .38 in a steady two-handed grip and fired.

The single shot dropped Farty suddenly as if he had tripped at full speed over a stretched taut wire.

'Christ, sir, you've bloody killed him,' Tucker said, between admiration and shock.

It took him a few moments to reply.

He thought of Daddy Duffell horribly battered to death in the derelict house in Pratts Town. Of Peter Kitson's mangled face, his life saved by the merest chance.

He rose to his feet.

'Yes,' he said, 'looks as though I've put paid to one criminal.'

He shook his head.

'There'll be a lot to say at the inquiry.'

# 20

The Chief insisted that he should take some time off.

'It's not every day, Mr French, that an officer in my force kills a man. It has never happened before, in fact. Not to my knowledge. And we must get you some counselling. It's bound to be a shock. Bound to be.'

'Well, sir, I think I would like to take a day or two off duty. Get away for a bit. But I don't know about the counselling. As far as I can see I was doing no more than my duty. There was a piece of criminal scum like Farty Corrigan firing a weapon in the vicinity of a party of innocent civilians, children among them. I've nothing to reproach myself with.'

'I dare say not, Mr French. I dare say not. Of course, the inquiry . . . However, we'll jump that fence when we come to it. And the press has been on to me. Elements of the press. I hadn't meant to mention it. But I suppose you must hear sooner or later. And what they call a researcher from that *Justice Watch* programme. Of course, I had no difficulty in dealing with them. Full inquiry, I said, in accordance with regulations. But the day will come . . .'

'As I said when I first reported to you, sir, there's nothing to be swept under any carpets. The media always like to get hot under the collar when someone's killed by a police officer, whatever kind of a shit it was.'

'Yes, well, that's— But off you go now – er – Ned. And after the coming weekend, say, we'll see how you feel about some psychiatric advice. No shame in it, you know. None at all. I'd take it willingly myself.'

If, you old fart, you ever got anywhere near doing what has to be done.

But all the same he needed a little time for certain affairs of his own.

So as soon as he got back to his office he asked Shirley to find out the times of trains to Nottingham. Somehow he didn't fancy the long car drive. Alone.

And too bad if the little bitch guessed why he wanted to go to Nottingham. If she dared say anything, he could always stamp on it with something about seeing his solicitor over new demands from long-ago divorced Myrtle.

But there was one other thing to do down there before going to see Deborah. Something he had to find out. Urgently.

'You seem to be making a habit of finding your way back to Nottingham, Ned. It's really for the pleasure of talking with an old mate about past times?'

'No, Graham. All right, there is something you can tell me. Not to beat about the bush, it's Palmy. I hear he's been suspended. What's it for?'

Graham Vaughan's face provided him with an instant answer. The worst answer.

'Come on, tell. I'm bound to find out before long, right?'

'Yes. Yes, well, Ned, I suppose you are. As you seem to have guessed, it's that old Heather Jonas business. Apparently Palmy, the stupid fool, got it into his head there was something in the woman's statement that would do him harm if it ever came to light. So he just went to the basement files and pinched it. Would have got away with it in the general run of things. But it so happened a young PC was on duty there who Palmy had played some sort of dirty trick on. And this lad began to wonder why a notorious do-nothing like Palmy was

194

busying himself going through way-back-in-time files. Kept a discreet eye on him. Saw him take something. Stuff it under his coat. So he checked up on what it had been.'

Might have known bloody Palmy'd make a balls of it.

'I see. So in due course your bright young PC, all of a worry, tells someone. That someone gets Internal Affairs on to it. Yes?'

'Exactly. They gave Palmy's flat a spin, soon as they heard. Found that statement tucked in a sealed container in the toilet cistern. First place they looked.'

Of course. Trust Palmy to do the easiest thing. Never mind all the experience he had.

'Par for the course with Palmy.'

'Ned, you look sick as a parrot. Is this going to do you serious harm?'

'Quite frankly, Graham, yes, it is. Serious as you can imagine.'

He went round to Deborah's flat as soon as she had been able to get away from the office. She produced whisky.

'Well, tell me about what happened there at Obelisk Hill,' she said. 'I only know what I read in the paper. They mentioned no police names. So who was it who actually shot that man Francis Corrigan? He was the one you called Farty, right?'

'It was me.'

'But— But do you want to tell me about it? Or . . .'

A few moments' thought. What to talk about first? In the end he decided on the least worrying.

'Okay, I'll tell you about it. I rather welcome the chance of talking to someone who won't be hostile. Or, on the other hand, won't just ooze meaningless sympathy.'

'Well, I'm sorry but I'll find it difficult to offer sympathy. You must know, I'm scarcely likely to approve unreservedly of something like that.'

195

'Oh, yes, I know. I mean, I did once sit on the other side of a desk from mind-made-up Ms Brooke.'

'Okay. But, remember, I was the one who once had a long conversation with a high-ranking police officer who in his early days had flagrantly committed a serious disciplinary offence. And I agreed to let the rules be bent in his favour. Just so that he could go ahead and catch his pet-hate criminals, as he says, bang to rights.'

So no delay in coming to Subject Number Two. The tougher one.

He gathered himself together.

'Yes. Yes, you did agree to hold your tongue. And— And it meant a lot to me. Though in the end it turns out it was all unnecessary.'

'Not necessary? What— What do you mean?'

'Just this. Internal Affairs up at Headquarters here caught on to Palmy taking Heather's statement out of the files. That's why he's been suspended, as we feared. And, I've no doubt, before very long he'll start claiming he only did what he did because of pressure from me. Then I'll be up in front of them. Less time than it takes to tell.'

'And— Ned, does that mean you'll be suspended yourself?'

'Of course. Suspended. Perhaps forced to resign. Perhaps charged with a number of offences.'

'Christ, Ned. Isn't there anything you can do?'

'To interfere with the course of justice? More than I have already? I don't think so, Ms Brooke.'

'But, Ned . . . Ned, you're a good detective. A bloody good detective. Look at the way you dealt with the Corrigans. Ned, they can't do this to you.'

'They can, you know. And they will. And you ought to be cheering them on. If you believe half what you've told me you believe.'

'I do. But—'

'But what?'

196

'Well, nothing, I suppose. Nothing.'

A silence.

Then she looked up.

He found it hard to read her expression. A bleak look of even darker despair.

'Ned. Ned, I must say this too. Ned, I've been reading a lot in the papers about— About Obelisk Hill. Some of it hinting it was a matter of taking the law into police hands. Ned, I want you to tell me what exactly happened out there. Did Farty Corrigan really deserve to be shot down? That's an altogether different matter from whether it was right to get the whole lot of them the way you did. I'm willing to agree that you were right then. Probably right. But killing Farty, that's what I want to hear you justify.'

'All right then, I'll go into full detail. We'd rounded up the whole bunch of them, and not before Barty Corrigan had attempted to take an innocent bystander woman hostage and had threatened to kill her. In front of her children.'

'So then you shot his brother, his cousin, whatever?'

'No. I don't say that I wouldn't have liked to. To have shot all three, all four of them. But I would never have done it, not unless they were actually threatening a life.'

'And was Farty doing that when you killed him? I thought you said they were all rounded up.'

'They were. Only Farty, in just the way I'd warned my team he might, succeeded in getting away again. He took to his heels, and went haring down the road. In the same direction as the wretched family were running for their lives. Quite unnecessarily, as a matter of fact.'

'And Farty running in the same direction constituted a threat to them? Is that what you're saying?'

'No. No, it isn't. Farty had grabbed a gun from the DC who was about to handcuff him and he was firing it.'

197

'I see. Well then, I suppose you were in fact justified in shooting at him yourself.'

He did not answer at once. No answer was really called for. But at last he spoke again.

Something impelled him to. To put in front of her, this woman he had mysteriously come to love, what his creed was. What it meant. Without the least misty veiling.

'The truth is there was hardly any chance of Farty's shots hitting those people. He'd no idea how to use a gun. He was simply loosing off. More or less into the air. And I could see it, though no one else was near enough to. I could see it. I knew just how much of a danger he was to those people. And I knelt down, took careful aim and fired at him. The shot might not have killed him, but I meant it to. That man had brutally murdered a silly old petty criminal on my patch. He'd damn nearly battered to death the snout I had, the one you met. Half met. No, he deserved to be killed, and I'm not ashamed that I killed him.'

'The good detective.'

The bitterness jetted out.

He had expected nothing less. But he made one last attempt to make her see. Make her agree.

'Yes, the good detective. Look at him. He's here now. In front of you. Telling you who he is. What he is. The one who does the dirty work. The dirty work that has to be done. Has to be done while there are scum like the Corrigans there. As there always will be, you know. Always will be. In just the same way that I shall always be there. Even after I've been made to resign. Been jailed even. People like me will be there. To do that dirty work. To keep it all clean. Or clean as it can be kept. For people like you. The ones who can go about saying, *Be tolerant. See the other point of view.* Yes, there'll be the intolerant ones there, the ones you need. A few of them. Always.'

'I— I suppose so.'

She fell silent, no longer looking at him but down at the carpet at her feet.

'Ned,' she said at last, 'you know I can never— I can never now make that permanency with you we thought about. Talked about. You know that, don't you? I had thought we could. I wanted to. God, how I wanted to. To get formally married, the whole thing. And I think you wanted it, too. I know you did. But, no. I see now, it can't be. It can never be. Not now. Not ever.'

## About the Author

H. R. F. Keating is one of Britain's most highly acclaimed crime novelists. He has twice won both the Gold Dagger Award from Britain's Crime Writers' Association and the Edgar Allan Poe Award from the Mystery Writers of America. One of his Gold Dagger winners, *The Perfect Murder*, was also made into a film by Merchant Ivory.

A graduate of Trinity College, Dublin, H. R. F. Keating worked as a journalist before becoming a full-time writer. He was the chief mystery reviewer for the London *Times* for fifteen years and has written numerous books on the genre including *The Bedside Companion to Crime*.

A former chairman of the Crime Writers' Association and the Society of Authors, Keating has since won election to the prestigious Detection Club and has served as the group's president. He is married to the actress Sheila Mitchell and lives in London.